I0671385

The Pale Titan

The Convergence Saga

Book 1

by

Rick Kueber

Contributing Photographer and
Model Photography- Tabitha Linton

Cover Model - Alyssa Evelyn Hutchison

Book Cover Design - Annette Munnich

Copyright © 2015
Stellium Books
www.stelliumbooks.com
Grant Park Illinois 60940
All Rights Reserved

ISBN: 978-0692611005
Manufactured in the USA

Dedication

As always this book is dedicated to my son Daniel,

but also to Annette for all of her hard work and dedication and Tabitha whose creative soul inspired me to create something unique and beautiful.

Chapter Index

The Pale Titan

The Pale Titan

The Pale Titan

CHAPTER 1

FIELD MOUSE

The night winds whipped cool around my bare back and neck as I stared out across the vast desert wastelands and the star filled sky. Being from Indiana, and never traveling any farther west than St. Louis, the confusion set in. Had it not been for a nearby cactus, I could have been on the surface of a distant planet for all I knew. Peering over my shoulder at the desolate mountains rising behind me, I wondered how I came to be here. Where was I? Had I come down from the mountains, or over them? Had I turned to face the daunting desert hell behind me, before turning back to face the mountainous terrain ahead? The only thing I was certain of was that I did not like the place where I found myself. My body ached, and my bare feet stung in the gritty sand and stones. I spun around and around hoping for some familiar landmark that would jar my memory, but there was nothing. Fear and solitude were gaining control of my mind and my attitude.

"Why am I here?" My shout echoed in the emptiness that surrounded me. A distant lone 'yip' of a coyote was the only response to my question. Could this be a dream? No, you can't feel in a dream, can you? Thoughts and questions bombarded my consciousness. A fleeting idea hit me and my hands slammed into my front pockets with earnest speed and force. I had hoped to find something, a receipt, note, ticket stub, some shred of evidence to explain why I found myself in this abyss. Nothing. Empty...like my stomach and my heart. I was living the metaphor of my own existence. I had nothing. I had no one. I was alone.

Looking in every direction, I tried to find proof of which way I had come, but the gusting winds had erased any trace of my path through the desert sands. I pulled at my hair, racking my brain to decide which way I should go. I let reason take over though there was nothing rational about this situation which I was now a part of. When I came to the realization of where I was, I had been facing the barren mountains with my back to the desert. I decided that was the direction I would go. Surely there would be some place civilized on the other side of the mountains if my path did not cross one as I traversed through them.

I was not particularly thirsty, but I was quite hungry, which was a conundrum, finding myself in a desert. I trudged ahead toward the looming giants, contemplating this enigma. What could this all mean? I may never know though I hoped I would live long enough to try to find the answers. Something unexpectedly caught my attention. A bright light swept across the sky above the mountaintop closest to me.

"Yes!" I screamed with excitement, "DOWN HERE!!" I waved my heavy arms over my head though I was nearly positive no one would be able to see me. The brightness of this light and its movement led me to a few possible conclusions. Perhaps it was from some sort of airport runway, or helicopter pad. Maybe it was a searchlight, being used as a signal by someone who knew I was lost.

I found my energy renewed as the adrenaline pulsed through my veins. My steps quickened as I approached the rocky terrain ahead. I lost my footing as the sand became more rocky and unstable. I slipped on the loose rocks and landed hard on my right side, scraping my palm, raising a goose egg on my shin and opening a sizable gash through my khakis and on the side of my calf. Whoever was operating this light may not have any answers for me. They may not know who I was, or why I was lost in this desert so far from my home, but there was one thing I felt sure of. Whoever this was, they could most certainly help me, and at least, offer me some food, water, first aid, and maybe get me in touch with the local authorities.

The occasional accelerated wind caused a chill as the blood ran down my leg. The stinging of the open wound gave me a new fear to think about... what if I couldn't make the climb to the top? Would I become fodder for a pack of coyotes? I stuck my fingers into the ripped opening in my pant leg and pulled with all of the strength I could muster. A few grunts, groans, and rips later and I had a makeshift khaki bandage wrapped tight around my calf.

I struggled to my feet and made a poor attempt to walk. The pain was quite intense and caused my body to tremble. I had been so stupid and careless to have let this happen. I hobbled forward step by step, assured that if someone saw me their first impression would be that they were experiencing the inception of the zombie apocalypse. I laughed at myself through the pain.

Pushing forward, the foot of the mountain was less steep than it appeared from only a few hundred yards away. Much to my surprise, I found the foothills to actually harbor some sparse vegetation and brush, which now seemed to become denser in places as I began my ascent. Finding a flat rock, some seven or eight foot across, I laid down to rest and stared up at the cruel night sky.

The silence was deafening, save for the occasional sound of the wind. I was unsure how long I had rested there, ten minutes or two hours, listening to the wind and what may have been the quick and quiet movement of a desert lizard or kangaroo rat scurrying in the underbrush and tumbleweeds. I listened more intently as the sounds became more frequent. The scuttling sounds grew closer, and the wind began to whisper to me... or perhaps to itself. I rolled onto my side away from my damaged leg.

"Don't move." A quiet, slow voice whispered to me from the darkness. Though I could not see where the voice came from, I dared not move.

A zzzzzzipping-hissssing sound and a sudden thud... I flinched and jerked, despite my warning not to move, when sand sprayed in my face from the swinging of the large stick, like a golf club in a sand trap, when it made contact with the sand, stones, and the sidewinder rattlesnake that was poised just a few short feet from where I rested.

"Stay still, or I **will** shoot you." Said the whispery voice. "Who are you?"

"I'm.... I'm Tanner. Tanner Astin." I surprised myself. I thought hard and realized that I knew my name, somehow I knew I was from Indiana, not far from the Illinois state line, and then things became very blurred. Just a few hours earlier, my questions were 'Where am I and why am I here?' now I found myself wondering 'Who am I?'. I was coming to the realization that I knew nothing about my past or present, and *that* was a disturbing feeling.

"Well, Tanner Astin, if that is who you really are, you need to come with me before they locate you." The voice whispered as I felt the cold metal of a gun barrel push against my shoulder as a gesture for me to move. I slowly stood up, hopping a bit to one side to avoid putting direct pressure on my lame, damaged leg.

"Aw, Hell! Half naked was bad enough, but you're hurt too?" The voice growled. "I should have just left you there with the rattlers."

"Yeah, you can still leave me here if you want, but I would really appreciate it if you didn't." I felt like I was respectfully begging for my life with as much dignity as I could muster. "Is it wrong to ask your name?"

"Yes, it is wrong." The voice was softer now, and less frustrated than before. "Elle."

"Huh, I'm sorry, I missed that last part," I whispered.

"Elle, my name is Elle." She said, and for the first time through the darkness, I could see that my captor, or my savior, dressed in tight black clothing that covered every inch of her body right up to the jaw line, was a woman. Her hair fell just past her shoulders, mostly one length as far as I could tell, and the ratted, tangled blackness of it told me that she had not seen a shower in days, probably longer. Bushy frizz and fringe covered most of her face giving her the appearance of near invisibility in the moonless desert night.

"My apologies Elle, but where are we going, or maybe I should ask, where are you taking me?" The puzzling amnesia had, at least, left my manners.

"Quiet!" She whispered forcefully and pointed ahead towards the rising cliff wall of the plateau before us.

I trudged along as best as I could and though no words were spoken, I could sense her frustration and something else... fear. Thirty minutes into the hike, we had climbed a fairly easy eighty feet in altitude when she suddenly stopped holding one hand up to silently signal me. I stopped dead in my tracks and tried to hide my labored breathing. Standing still for a few moments while she scanned the area using some type of large binoculars, the pain in my leg began to take effect. The hiking, climbing and trying to keep up with Elle had not been ideal for mending the puncture to my calf, in fact, I was certain I had done much more damage than good.

Elle motioned me to move in front of her and I, once again, felt the cold steel of the rifle barrel on my skin. The prodding pressure on my back coerced me to take the lead. I took a few slow steps holding my hands out in front of me, not raised in surrender, but to help avoid running into anything in what had become a near pitch black night. I could feel her body occasionally brushing up against me from behind. Her pointed finger would jut past my shoulder every few steps pointing me in the direction of her desire. She laid her hand on my shoulder and I felt compelled to stop. She pressed herself against me from behind and I could feel the length of the rifle against my back and her breath in my ear as she softly whispered, "In."

I glanced around as my eyes adjusted to the lack of light and noticed we had stopped against the cliff wall I had seen from the distance. A few tumbleweeds had blown against a rugged banzai looking shrub that grew out of the sharp corner where the cliff wall met our path. Looking over my shoulder, I questioned what she meant by 'in' without uttering a sound. She kicked at one of the tumbleweeds and pushed down forcibly on my shoulder and I clumsily made my way to the ground. On my hands and knees, I crawled into a mysterious foxhole. The hole and tunnel that followed were not much bigger than I was. I had to pull myself along with my elbows and hands. There was a pain as I felt her boot slide hard against my bare feet. She had slid in feet first and the only sense I could make of it was that she was pulling the tumbleweeds back into their place to disguise the entrance to the wormhole we were crawling through. After a series of turns and a raising and lowering of the tunnel floor, I could see the hint of a light ahead. It was very dim, but I found it comforting. I reached a cloth of some sort which was covering the tunnel and allowed only a small amount of light to pass through. I paused only for a moment when I felt an abrupt boot tread kick to my heel. I scurried forward on my belly past the cloth into a bright opening. I could hear shuffling as someone, or maybe more than one someone, scattered. Once I was clear of the tunnel I rolled onto my back and got my first glimpse of my surroundings.

The tiny tunnel had opened into a cave of some size. Nearly twenty foot in diameter and a ceiling of probably ten foot at its highest point, the entirety of the cave was lit by one lantern. Though compared to daylight, it was dim and dank, it seemed rather luminous compared to the only reality I could remember. Splashed against the stone walls were three young children and another young woman.

Elle popped through the tunnel opening and with the snap of a gymnast was on her feet next to me. I lay there on my back looking up at my captor/ savior and attempted a pained smile.

"So. Tanner...who are you, and just what the hell were you doing out there screaming? You have some sort of death wish?" Elle's voice was just above a whisper now and sounded more female than it had since we had met just a short time ago. The ground beneath me trembled like a small aftershock of an earthquake. My eyes darted around nervously, but not even the children seemed to notice or pay attention to the tremor.

Her words confused me and I replied in the only way I knew how. "I..I don't know who I am really. I think I'm from Indiana. I have no idea how I got to this desert, or why I have no shirt or shoes. I just sort of *woke up* standing there in the sand and wind." I could tell my words felt empty and hollow to her, and I could sense there was a hesitation to believe me. "Not sure why you think I have a death wish, just the opposite really. I just wanted to be found."

The tremor buzzed the earth beneath me once again, and I blurted out, "Didn't you all feel that?"

"SHHHHH!" the children hushed me.

"You do have a death wish, don'tcha?" muttered the other woman under her breath.

Elle leaned into me and whispered sternly. "I'm not sold on your story...yet...but as much as you wanted to be found, you're damn lucky I found you and not them."

My eyes grew open wide and met Elle's. They were hardened, but deep inside their muddy brownness, I could see there was a kindness she kept hidden from the harsh world outside. Who were 'they' and why shouldn't I want them to find me. Why were we all hiding in this rat hole in the ground? Whether I wanted them or not, I needed these questions answered. These answers might not tell me who I am, or why I am here, but they might help me understand my current situation, and why these five women and children harbored the need to hide beneath the ground, cowering like field mice always in fear of the barn cats poised to make a quick and bloody meal of them, or tear their heads off and bring them back as trophies to their master.

I slowly raised my hand and touched Elle on the arm gently. "Please, tell me."

"Tell you what?" there was a slight squeak in her voice as she spoke this time, like a deeply buried emotion was trying to escape through the callous shell formed by the difficult life she had.

I wrapped my hand around her forearm and gave a gentle squeeze as I spoke. "Everything.... I want to know everything." I lowered my eyes to the dimly lit earth below us as the faintest of tremors buzzed once again. "Please? Who are we hiding from?"

"Tomorrow," she whispered softly. Her hand reached up longingly and her fingers brushed my cheek. "You need rest. We all do. Sleep now, before the sun rises, and we will talk again when we wake." Subtlety was something Elle had mastered, but I could read her emotions already. She cared, and that calmed my nerves. I began to believe I could sleep.

Elle motioned to the other woman. "This is Tory," She said as the other woman handed a bundle of heavy fabric to me.

"Hi." was all she whispered to me and then jerkily turned her head and returned to the children on the other side of the cave.

"There is a piece of thick fleece that will make a good blanket for you. It gets pretty cool in here, even during the day. And there is another piece tied up that you can rest your head on. That's enough for the time being. If you can't sleep, or you find you are the only one awake, whatever you do, do not go outside...." She rustled her fingers through my hair, and I wondered if she thought of me like one of the feral children she was protecting. "...now sleep."

"I will try to rest. Thanks." I said, and I meant it wholeheartedly, even though I had no idea how thankful I should be. I spread the fleece out on the ground and placed the makeshift pillow at one end. I stretched out on one side of the blanket and placed my head on the pillow, pulling the covers over me. I relaxed easily and the hard dirt somehow made a comfortable resting place. Though my mind raced, it wasn't long before I fell asleep.

CHAPTER 2

THE TAKER

I awoke with a start, rolling over and swiftly jerking my head side to side. A lone candle painted a pale glow on the cavern walls in places and caused shadows to dance in the recesses. My leg ached. It was not the sharp shooting pain of yesterday, but a duller aching that radiated more evenly from the point of my puncture wound. Looking around, I slowly sat up as silently as I could manage. I saw one of the women curled up against the opposite wall, and the three children sprawled out in various states of disarray. I had a flash from my past. It felt very distant as I recalled seeing several youngsters sleeping on a carpeted floor in disorder as a television played cartoons quietly in the background. The memory was gone, but I had a comforting and saddening feeling that I had a life somewhere far from here.

I sat there contemplating my life with no real memories, and what the world had become. What was there to learn from

Elle, that she didn't want to tell me last night? Day and night had become confusing to me. Hidden in this sandstone grave, I was unsure if it was light or dark outside or what time it was. There was one thing that was most prevalent on my mind. Where was Elle?

One of the children began to stir and soon all three were awake. Their first task after waking was to wake up the slumbering woman. She awoke surprisingly happy and I noticed the volume of their conversations were notably louder than they had been before we slept.

"Do you know where Elle is?" I asked in a gentle tone, so as to not startle them.

"Not sure, I just woke up... but you knew that already," she said. She crossed the cave on her hands and knees as she spoke. Stopping just short of where I sat, she extended her hand and I gently grasped it and gave her a friendly shake. "I'm Tory, and those three are Jamie, Josh, and Maddie. Maddie's seven and she's mine."

I waved over Tory's shoulder to the children, two girls and a boy, and then looked back to Tory. "Pleased to meet you, Tory. I'm Tanner." I paused a moment before adding, "...And I'm.... hungry. I don't suppose there is any extra food around, is there?"

"We have a little bit of food and water, but you will have to wait and ask Elle when she returns, it's really hers." Tory answered as the expression on her face went blank. There was a sinking feeling in my gut that she wasn't altogether sure when or if Elle would ever return.

I leaned back against the cave wall, sticking my makeshift pillow behind my neck and let out an audible sigh. Tory moved to the far right rear of the cavern and retrieved a nap sack. She shuffled through it occasionally shooting a quick glance at me over her shoulder. I closed my eyes and pretended to be oblivious to her actions. Returning to the children, I peeked through nearly closed eyes to see her hand them each something wrapped in shiny metallic cellophane. I watched enviously as the children opened the wrappers and began devouring some type of granola or cereal bars. My stomach clenched and ached with hunger. I could not remember the last time I ate. In all honesty, I couldn't remember ever eating.

As the kiddos played amongst themselves, Tory split her attention between them and me. I felt like I was being babysat, so I slumped back over and rested trying to ignore the pain in my leg and Tory's random stares. I wasn't certain if she was afraid of what I might do, or if she was feeling guilty after feeding the youngsters, but not me.

Something brought me back from near unconsciousness. At first, I thought it was the tremors from earlier, but I soon came to the realization that someone was coming through the diminutive entrance. First hands and arms, swiftly followed by the head and face of Elle. She pulled herself in with the quick grace of a gymnast, spinning around and landing on her feet, poised in a crouching position.

"You're back," I stated with a voice that was dry and cracked though it almost sounded like a question.

"I always come back," she replied, pulling a small pack off of her shoulder and casting a smile to the kids and Tory. "It's quiet out there. Time to move."

"Where to?" Tory inquired.

"Not far. With his hurt leg, maybe three hours...probably five hours or more till the sun goes down." The children froze and they stared at Elle wide-eyed. I recognized the fear in them and it unnerved me.

Elle pointed to me, then the children and finally Tory. Then cupping her hand she motioned us to follow her. One by one we inched our way out of the hole and into the bright daylight. The sun was high in the cloudless blue sky and caused my eyes to water in it glare. We gathered outside and Tory whispered to Elle. Elle nodded back, looking at me. I feared what they were agreeing about. Perhaps I was about to be left behind due to my gimpy leg. I was pondering the possibilities when I saw Elle reach slowly into her pack, her eyes never leaving me. Did she have a gun, a knife... was I about to be permanently left behind? Surely not in front of the children. Elle drew her hand from the pack and pointing it in my direction, handed me one of the sacred, granola bars.

"Thank you." I mouthed silently. Everyone smiled. Elle swiftly turned and motioned us again.

We followed her down a path that was visible only in Elle's head. Though we weren't completely hiding, we did remain cautious to not be obtrusive. The aching in my leg grew more uncomfortable with each step and after about an hour and a half, I tugged at Elle's pack.

"Can we rest? Just for a minute, please?"

Stopping short, she held up her hand and with fingers spread said, "Five-minute break, and then we move again."

Everyone sat down right where we were, and I broke the silence once again. "You were going to tell me... everything... when we got up. What are we hiding from? What is everyone so frightened of?" Tory glared at me and the children gasped and slapped their hands over their mouths.

"We are hiding from the Titans, and what are we frightened of? The Ahsusha." As Elle spoke these names, the children hid their faces and Tory looked around uneasily. "Are you afraid to die Tanner?"

"I suppose I am. Are you?"

"No. I am afraid of being taken by the Ahsusha and not dying." Her voice quivered, and for the first time, I could see a hidden vulnerability.

"Okay, I realize I have some form of amnesia, but I really have no clue what you are talking about. The only Titans I know of are a football team and a group of teenage comic book heroes, and I never heard of anything called an Ahsusha."

19

"When we get to the camp, you will know all we know. For now, just know we are all being hunted. Some are rabbits and mice meandering around aimlessly, a few of us are more like wolves, built to survive and ready to fight for our lives... but we are all still being hunted." And with that Elle slung her pack over her shoulder and stood up. The rest of us quickly followed suit.

"What kind of camp are we headed to?" I asked with a hopeful demeanor.

"There are a dozen people, including us now, that are holding up at a mountain retreat. Used to be a vacation time-share or something. It's just a couple of rustic cabins, but there are real beds, baths, and until the gas runs out, we can cook and take warm baths. You'll see how it works when we get there."

We traveled along slowly as the terrain became more challenging and the greenery grew denser as we journeyed into a canyon. Sheer walls towered on three sides, and actual trees, though mostly conifers, began to fill our surroundings.

"Over there! It's a road!" I shouted and was immediately bashed upside of my head with Elle's pack and her enraged stare.

Elle over animatedly mouthed silently to me, "What-the-fuck?"

I held my arms out and looked from side to side as if to respond with 'What did I do?', when I realized we stood alone. Tory and the children were nowhere to be seen. I spun around once and instantly felt Elle's hand forcefully pushing down on the side of my head, neck, and shoulder. I fell hard, and the pain in my leg shot through me like an electric jolt.

Elle fell on top of me throwing her blanket/poncho completely over us. I could feel her breath in my ear and her pounding heartbeat against my bare back, fast and heavy at first. A few moments passed... silent, motionless moments when Elle whispered in my ear scarcely louder than a breath.

"If you want to be the bunny shouting, 'come eat me!' that's up to you, but I'll be damned if you are getting anyone else killed."

"Sorry. I'm just so confused still. I don't want anyone to die. Especially me."

"Well, if it will help, I can duct tape your mouth for the rest of our hike, but I hate to waste the tape. I don't want to do anything *drastic*, but I will do what I have to to survive."

"No. I will keep silent. I promise."

"Good... 'cause I kinda like having you around, Tanner Astin."

I smiled silently, and lay still, enjoying the closeness of my new, and possibly only, friend. Though we were still and silent as the dead for nearly ten minutes, I felt her body relax and melt against mine. It was a pleasant surprise since I thought I might be gutted for being such an idiot when Elle initially slammed me to the hard dirt and pine needles.

Cautiously, she began to draw back the burlap poncho that covered us, until our heads were revealed enough to take in our surroundings. Slowly, she divided us, standing up, sliding her rifle from shoulder to hands. Placing the stock of the rifle to her shoulder, she scanned our surroundings. When her stare reached the area where I had spotted the road, she raised the barrel and took aim. My heart raced like never before. We had played the quiet mouse game since this reality had started for me, and suddenly Elle was prepared to shatter the silence and give us away.

Her glare turned from her gun sights to me. With a stern look, she puckered her lips and gave me a silent 'shhh'. Taking her finger from the trigger, she waved me up. I raised my eyebrows and widened my eyes at her as if to say... 'I don't know how quiet I can be'. I held my breath and took as many seconds as I needed to gain my composure and stand.

Elle stood statuesque except for her trigger hand. I moved silently behind her. She touched the nearest gun sight with her pointer finger and slowly slid it forward down the barrel, slightly lifting as she did, until she was pointing to a distant point. Following her direction, I studied the distance. Through the trees and beyond the many boulders and obstacles before us lay the road, and then I saw it. Movement. It was a person, slowly trudging up the incline of the paved drive. At this distance, I couldn't tell if they were hurt, tired, sick, or just lost, but their movement was slow and awkward. Elle painstakingly lowered the gun.

She turned conservatively toward me, leaning her face on the side of my head and whispered directly into my ear. "Taker, maybe Ahsusha...can't tell from this distance. It's in the eyes, and the marks." I could feel the fear in her trembling voice.

We stood motionless for what felt like an eternity. My legs ached and I gritted my teeth through the painful sensations. In time, I felt her begin to relax her tensed muscles and I did the same. This 'Taker' had been gone for quite some time and had followed the road until disappearing from our sight. He had been gone and there had been no sign of any other movement for such a long time that I had lost track of how long we stood there. The entire time I wondered and worried. What was the purpose of a Taker, and had Tory and the children fallen prey to this person, or thing?

"Time to go." She said hurriedly and continued in the direction we had been going, which was, for all intents and purposes, the same direction as the Taker had gone.

"Wait a minute." I reached up and took Elle by the arm, wrapping my hand around her bicep. "What about Tory, and the kids, and why are we heading the same way as that Taker?"

"If they're okay, they'll find us. And as far as the Taker, where there is one, there have usually been many more, many more. We have to try to get to the camp before it does. I hope you are up to moving as quickly as you can and still be quiet." Her expression saddened. "Trust me, please?"

The way she called the taker '*it*' left a cold, eerie, and empty feeling in my chest. "You have probably saved my life more times than either of us knows. Of course, I trust you." At that moment, I wondered how many people Elle had saved and how many she had lost. "How long has this been going on?"

She shot a queer look in my direction before finally speaking. "Oh, yeah... Amnesia. About three weeks I guess." She mustered a half smile. "When we get to the camp, I will tell you everything I know."

"You promise? I've heard this before, and I'm still lost as to what the hell is really going on." I smiled.

"Tell you what... If we get to the camp, and it's not total chaos, I will tell you everything I know, and a few things I don't....Promise." She winked at me and took off towards the camp.

I struggled to keep up as we climbed higher, and delved deeper into the canyon. Making our way over a collection of fallen boulders of various sizes, Elle grabbed my hand and helped me up and over. Feeling a reversal of roles, I thanked her when she helped me down the other side. Without releasing my hand, she pulled me down next to her behind our rocky plethora, and put her finger to her lips, to shush me. We sat quietly and listened intently to the deafening silence. Then the slightest of noises caught our attention. The rustling of steps on the stones, twigs, and leaf litter on the floor of the canyon only yards from us. Elle raises the rifle into its place and aimed it up in the direction we had come. The scuffling sounds came from the other side of the landslide boulders. I tensed instinctively as Elle drew down on her sights, trigger finger twitching as she squeezed and released against the trigger, preparing to fire if necessary. The sounds grew closer, though still carefully quiet. Elle eased up on her grip, slightly lowered her aim, and loosened her composure as Tory peaked the boulders, followed by all three little ones.

I exhaled deeply and raised my hand in acknowledgment to the foursome. Elle and I stood up, and when the others reached us, we greeted them with hugs. It was amazing how close I felt to these strangers I had only met a day ago and had hardly even spoken to. I suppose there were obvious reasons since I had no memory of anyone else, Elle had saved my life, and they had all taken me in, like a stray puppy.

After our reunion, we hiked at a fast and steady pace to make up for lost time until we could see the first of the two cabins in the distance. Closing in on the cabin, we began to see the gathering of people outside, milling around.

CHAPTER 3

CRASH OF THE TITANS

The introductions were swift and quiet, which was exactly what I had expected. There was only one other child there, a young teen named Todd. I was introduced to an older, 60-something couple who had been the actual tenants of the cabin before the arrival of the Ahsusha, Mel and Irene, another couple Mark and Darcy, parents probably, dark hair, eyes and olive skin that gave them the appearance of being foreign, though they spoke with no accent whatsoever. The other three were two women and a young man all in their twenties, by my guess, Maya, Ally, and Trevor.

My head was abuzz trying to remember so many new names and faces at once. Elle pulled the four of us inside one of the cabins with her and showed us around the kitchen and then the bathroom where I spied the tub. Heaven on earth is what I saw, and as much as I wanted to soak and wash the grime out of my wound and my hair, I offered to let the ladies and children take their turns first. Elle let Tory and Jamie take the first turn in the tub and then went to the kitchen while I quickly located the sofa and took the load off of my leg.

"Oh my god!" I exclaimed at a reasonable volume. "I forgot what it felt like to be comfortable!"

Elle emerged from the kitchen with two paper plates and a can of soda. She handed one of the plates to me and sat down comfortably close to me. The peanut butter sandwich was a delicacy that I thoroughly enjoyed to the last delectable crumb, and though I have never been a fan of diet drinks, the diet, Dr. Pepper, I shared with Elle was magnificent. By the time we had finished, Tory and Jamie emerged from the bath, wrapped in towels and carrying soaking wet, dripping clothes in their arms. Elle showed them where to hang their clothes to dry, and took them directly into one of the bedrooms. They all emerged with mismatched clothes that were apparently not the correct sizes. The disheveled look was quickly dismissed by the look of relief on their faces.

I relaxed as time passed slowly. A touch on my shoulder stirred me back from near unconsciousness. It was Elle, wrapped in a towel, black hair dripping, and appearing more like a wood nymph than a desert guerrilla. This was my first look at her face, not covered in the web of tangled hair and gritty dust. She was petite, with a naturally tanned skin tone, unlike me. I was typically either pasty white, or sunburned. From the waste up, the latter was fairly accurate.

"It's your turn. I hope there is still some warm water left," she smiled with a flirty grin as her fingertips slid down the length of my arm, brushing my thigh when she turned, walking toward the bedroom across from where I sat. I was mesmerized by her every move. When the bedroom door was closed to the point of being slightly cracked, she disappeared from sight. Her towel was tossed across the room and I watched as it flickered past the sliver of an opening. The teenage part of my libido urged me to cross the room and steal a peek of nirvana. I let the man in me prove that I had respect, and I left my place on the comfortable couch. The bath felt amazing on my parched, and dust-caked skin. It did sting the gash on my calf, but I didn't mind. I had lost track of time after cleaning every inch of my body at least once. I lay there in my own peaceful oblivion. The door opened abruptly and Elle's face popped through the opening.

"It will be dark soon. You need to get out and get dressed." She was almost blushing when I realized though the water had become rather dirty, I was quite exposed to her stare. "Here's a towel," she remarked as she broke her concentration, tossing a terry cloth bath towel to the edge of the tub. Her eyes had dropped to the floor, but I noticed one last glance up, and a smile, at my naked physique before disappearing and closing the door.

I emerged from the bedroom after dressing in what was obviously a golfing outfit, and cardigan socks. I had even found a pair of slip-on loafers that were only slightly snug. It was awkward, but at least, I felt somewhat civilized. Tory, Mark, and Darcy were sitting on the sofa, and Elle sat alone on the two cushioned love seat that jutted perpendicular to the end of the couch. I joined them, taking a seat next to Elle, who was dressed in a paisley printed green, tan and brown sundress. I tried not to stare at how the dress lay loose, yet melted against the tiny features of her body.

"Anyone else feel like a fire?" I asked breaking the silence of the room, and feeling a bit romantic, although I guessed that Tory may be feeling like a fifth wheel.

"No." answered Mark. "We can't."

I gave him a puzzled look, thinking a fire would be easy to build. I had seen plenty of dry fallen branches and kindling. "Why?"

Mark and Darcy looked at me curiously, but it was Elle who answered my question, giving them insight as to who I was also.

"Tanner has a strange case of amnesia. He doesn't understand the weight of our situation, and I promised him I would explain everything when we arrived here and were settled." The couple expressed emotion in their faces, sadness, fear, and worry.

"Tanner," Elle continued, "The Titans and the Ahsusha can sense heat signatures. The Titans, we think are equipped with some type of thermal imaging, and the Ahsusha... god, where do I begin?" She sighed, and rubbed her face bottom to top, then ran her spread fingers through her still damp hair, front to back. She slid her hands to her shoulders and left them there as she looked from one to another of my new acquaintances.

"Start from the beginning. You said something about them showing up a few weeks ago. Is that right?" I tried to be as straightforward as I could muster. "Just be honest, and don't spare any details, even the ones that are theories."

"Okay, here goes..." Elle crossed her hands on her lap and turned toward me. "It was a Tuesday. I was on vacation with my brother and his family. We had been to the Grand Canyon, and then traveled to just about ten miles from here in a rented R.V. We had parked it off the road, and gone out for a day hike, to do some exploring, climbing, and just to take in the amazing views of the Mojave desert."

"So that's where we are!" I exclaimed excited by the realization that I recognized these locations, but I was quickly hushed by three scowls from the couch. "Sorry." I almost whispered.

"It's okay, but we are still in danger, and the darker it get outside, the more the danger grows," Tory said, understanding my elation.

Elle continued. "It was growing later in the afternoon when we were making our decent. There was this sound like the thunder of a squadron of jet fighters and the pulsing 'thwap-thwap' of a military helicopter fleet. We searched the skies above us but saw nothing at first. We sat on a flat rock nearby and continued scanning the overcast skies. The sound was growing along with our concern, when my brother pointed to the horizon and shouted 'There, look there!' It was hard to believe that three small objects in the distance were making such a racket, but they drew closer, and their thumping and humming became nearly unbearable. The objects, were the Titans, and they glowed from their belly side, and smoke or contrails billowed behind like they were huge asteroids, crashing to earth. As they shot closer and closer their massive forms were daunting."

"We cowered with our hands over our ears as two of the three came crashing and sliding into the desert sands below us. The force caused the earth to quake with such strength that the side of the cliff we had been exploring crashed down around us. My brother's entire family was killed in the landslide."

I took Elle's hand and comforted her. She shed no tears, and I imagined what she must have seen since then to have caused her to have the strength to hold in such powerful emotions.

"When the third Titan, the pale one, cleared the plateau, we felt its impact shake the ground, but it must have fallen many miles away because it didn't cause the same magnitude of damage as the other two had. My brother and I scrambled to the bottom and peered from behind a few large fallen boulders. My brother, Bobby, rushed out from our hiding spot to get a better look. I grabbed at his shirt, but couldn't stop his curiosity. He ran out and vanished into the dusty cloud that rolled out from the impact zone. I watched as the cloud rolled in like a fog. I pulled off my t-shirt and covered my mouth, nose, and eyes...and I waited. I sat in silence for a long time. I began to hear the humming, like electricity through the high tension lines. It took forever for the dust and smoke to settle, but when it did, I was awestruck at the sight that took form before my eyes."

Elle paused for a minute, and Darcy asked, "Would anyone like a cold drink?"

"Cold, really? I would love one!" I looked at Elle. "Share one with me?" she nodded.

"They aren't really cold, but we found a storm cellar under this cabin. There is a trap door over here under the rug, and it's really cool down there, so we put most of the drinks down there yesterday. Not cold, but they are pretty refreshing."

I gave Elle the first drink and when she finished, she handed it to me and continued her recant.

"Well, there amidst the dust that still hung in the air, I could see what I can only describe as a trapezoid shaped, metallic dark blue structure. There were blackened smoky stains that radiated from underneath it and two circular and rectangular structures that ran across the lower half of the main 'trapezoid' on each side. They were ginormous, and I can only compare their size to a building the size of a football stadium, laying on its side. The sand had been melted into glass by the intense heat from their entering the atmosphere, and jutted out around them like inverted icicles, disfigured cone shapes the length of telephone poles, some longer."

Something Elle said caught me by surprise and I could feel the blood leaving my face as it paled. She said 'when they entered the atmosphere'. Was she really implying an alien invasion of some sort?

"Aliens, as in alien invasion?" I questioned.

"I don't know for sure, invasion gone wrong, or accidental. Maybe they were mistakenly caught in our gravitational pull and it caused them to come pummeling to earth by chance or mistake. From the scene of the landing, or crash, which is more accurate of a description, I don't think they meant to invade...at least not yet. Not like this.

Anyway, I stepped away from the stone barrier that I had hidden behind and went to find Bobby. I had journeyed about a hundred yards when I realized two things. One: they were much larger than a football stadium, and two: they had not been completely disabled in the crash. The sun was low on the horizon when the whirring and buzzing increased in speed. The sand beneath my feet vibrated nonstop, and the closer of the two titans began to move in a jerky, awkward motion. It started to rise off of the ground when I figured out the attached structures, the circular parts, were actually moving parts and the other rectangles were stretching out like the legs of a deformed robotic dog."

"YES! Exactly! Kinda like a monkey, I thought." Said Tory and everyone nodded in agreement.

"To shorten the tale, since I don't know how much time we have, both Titans raised up and very slowly turned towards the mountains. They took awkward step after step, and though their movements were slow, their immense size allowed them to cover a lot of distance in a fairly short time. One of them froze when a tour bus pulled over near our R.V. It appeared to sit like an obedient dog, and that's when I saw them for the first time.

A hoard of people clambered off of the bus to see the amazing Titans. An opening at the ground level had appeared and a dozen 'beings' exited the craft. The sun was almost completely gone and the sky was turning dark. These 'beings' were a translucent gray color and emitted a dull glow. They didn't light up the area around them, but they were easy to see in the darkening desert. They approached the stunned tourists, who just stood there like they were going to shake hands with the friendly little grays from that Close Encounters movie. The beings, the Ahsusha, did reach out to them, but their 'hugs, enveloped the people, one by one. They all just stood there like cattle as the Ahsusha absorbed the energy from one passenger at a time."

Elle paused only long enough to take the drink from my hand, wet her throat and hand it back to me. She placed her hand on my thigh as she continued.

"This part is a theory, but I think everyone who has had any encounter with them will agree it is a good theory, and as accurate as anyone from this planet can formulate." She was articulate, intelligent, strong, and beautiful. "The people didn't die, but it's like the humanity died in them. I rushed to a nearby outcropping of rock to hide and watch. After they had taken what they wanted from these people, they herded them into the Titan and it 'stood' back up and began its ground shaking trek up to and then over the mountain. Once it seemed clear, I ran to the R.V. and tried to make a getaway, you know, to tell somebody what was happening, but it wouldn't start. Dead battery. It was the same for the tour bus. I think it had something to do with the titans because I haven't come across anything battery powered that works since then, not even the flashlights in the R.V.

Anyway... I took off on foot from there and that's when I found these cabins and met Mel and Irene. They said there was a family staying in the other cabin that had gone sightseeing about twenty minutes before the crash. I told them to stay put, and I would try to find them... figured I would keep an eye out for Bobby too, but I already had a very bad feeling about him.

So, over the past couple of weeks, I have ventured out finding random people and bringing them back here. It was on one of those searches that I nearly stumbled upon an entire herd, like 20 people...or, at least, they used to be people. I saw one walking from a distance and thought it was someone who was hurt or dehydrated or something. I ran up to her, and I swear her eyes had gone completely pinkish red. No pupils, nothing, just this sickening pinkish red color. I tried to shake her, and that's when she grabbed my wrist and I couldn't believe her strength for someone who looked like a career crack head. You know the look, strung out, nappy hair, skin and bones, sunken cheeks... but she opened her mouth and aside from the horrid breath, she let out this low rumbling tone... almost like she was singing a very flat note that didn't fluctuate. She held it the entire time she had my wrist."

Elle paused for a moment to rub her eyes and take another drink. "Then I saw them over this woman's shoulder. The rest of them were quickly moving in my direction. I struggled to get away from her grip, but it was like her fingers were locked around my wrist like a handcuff. As the others drew near, I became frantic and could see two of them in the crowd were different. They were still the same crack headed, zombie looking people, but their eyes, they were illuminated. They had the same gray glow as the Ahsusha's entire bodies had. I panicked and then I did what was the most horrible thing I had ever done. I reached to my side and drew out this knife," she motioned as if actually retrieving a knife from its sheath, "and I swung it as hard as I could and cut her hand from her wrist. Blood sprayed everywhere, all over me, all over the ground, and her hand lost its grasp and fell. I turned and ran as the chorus of Takers, moaned in unison and followed after me. I hid and I watched them from afar, as they meandered up the road. I kept my distance, but I felt that somehow they knew I was there but had another, more important, agenda. I watched as they came to a camp area, and I looked on in horror as they rounded up men, women and children from their tents and campers and locking them in their grips, hurried them back to the road where they stood as the ground shook. One of the Titans was approaching from the south. I studied their actions, from my hiding spot, and that's when I saw one of the gray eyes standing apart from the rest. His eyes were actually glowing more intensely than before and suddenly, like jello, an Ahsusha came out of him. I don't know how to explain it exactly, but maybe it was like a ghost leaving a body of someone who had died. The host body of the man then crumpled to the ground like a pair of dirty discarded jeans or a bicycle inner tube with a hole in it, deflating, limp and lifeless."

"I came face to...whatever with one once," said Mark. "It was the creepiest thing I have ever seen, even in the movies. This thing had a mostly human form, but it was kind of bulkier, I dunno if that's a good way to describe it, but yeah, it was like a luminescent gray jello. I had my pistol, and I shot it right in the head. I guess it was the head, anyways.... kinda hard to tell...they don't have a face like we do, no eyes no mouth, no nothin', really creeped me out bad, but I pulled the trigger and I thought I blew its brains out, but it just kind of formed back together, and the little gray glowing bits that I blew everywhere, well, they just kinda made their way back to its body. It wasn't fazed at all. It reached out for me and moved in my direction with a handful of those takers.

I'm not particularly proud of it, but I shot four of them dead. It felt more like putting down a rabid dog, ya know? I was afraid of them, but it was kinda sad when they just dropped like somebody pulled the plug on one of those blow-up, holiday yard decorations. I managed to get away and was running for my life through the pines when Elle grabbed me, and I damn near shot her too."

Elle smiled at the tale and responded with, "You would have shot me if I wasn't such a bad-ass. I took that pistol from you with one hand." and the whole group of us smiled and chuckled under our breath.

Just then, Jamie rushed in the front door, and cringed into Tory's arms, pointing at the door. Mark, Elle, and I popped up from our seats and flew outside with total disregard for our own safety. "What's goin' on out here?" I shouted and then prepared for my reprimand from Elle, but she said nothing as we both focused on the teenaged boy Todd, who was holding up a coyote pup in one hand by its hind legs.

CHAPTER 4

THE GATHERING

Todd had a blank look on his face and quickly began his apology. "I didn't mean to scare her really. I just found this out there in the woods and thought it was cool. I ran back here to show everybody.. and I guess I almost hit that little girl with it when I came around that corner over there." He held back a laugh and pointed to the cabin across the clearing from us.

"Drop it," said a monotone voice. "How far away?" I was shocked to realize that the emotionless, robotic tone came from Elle, the woman I had just been daydreaming about earlier. She had been wrapped in a towel, soaking wet, whispering words that sounded like an angel. Suddenly she had turned into a cold huntress, and killer, at least, her voice had.

Todd dropped the pup where he stood, held his hands up and backed away. His face paled and worry clouded his expression. Elle swiftly approached it and began examining it thoroughly. She raised one of its limp eyelids to reveal a gray pupil-less eye, and turned her face to me, over her shoulder, with a concerned look. Frantically, she looked around and I could see her mouthing numbers as she counted.

"Get everyone inside this cabin, **now**!" Her voice never raised, but its intensity was such that it didn't need volume to get her point across. I made eye contact with everyone, waving my hand like a traffic cop to 'keep it moving' but with a little more haste. I too counted and checked faces as they passed, remembering who was left inside, and who was just sent in.

"Mel and Josh aren't here," I whispered to Elle.

"You check the other cabin, and I'm gonna check right around here and in the woods." She directed.

"Okay. Be careful." I said as I trotted up to the cabin porch.

"Always am." She whispered back and then vanished into the dusky twilight.

I emerged from the cabin a few moments later holding Mel by the upper arm and escorted him to the cabin. I was focused on my purpose, and probably seemed more like an angry cop pulling a detainee from his home and into custody than a friend, but I was acting in his best interest. I rushed him into the other cabin and counted faces once again. Two short, Elle and Josh. I spun around and darted for the door saying, "Wait here!"

Shooting out of the door and off of the rustic wooden porch in two long strides, I jumped to the ground. I stifled a guttural noise that tried to force its way out of me when I landed hard on the uneven ground and the discomfort of my injury immediately switched to a shooting pain. I composed myself and hobbled around the corner of the cabin and almost plowed over our two missing companions.

Once back inside the cabin, Elle began turning out the lights and blowing out all of the candles. "Get the blinds and curtains quick!"

Tory, Mark, Darcy and I made the rounds, haphazardly twisting blind rods and releasing the curtains from their tie backs until the cabin had gone dark. We carefully found our way back to the front room and took seats where we could find them.

"Alright," I huffed, out of breath from the rush of adrenaline and nerves, "new guy here... what's going on?"

"That pup was like a wet noodle, hadn't been dead long, and I found no marks on it anywhere. So, what's going on is this; There is an Ahsusha out there somewhere, probably too close for comfort...maybe that Taker we saw earlier. If they took the life from that pup that close to the cabins, they know we're here. No question." Elle was always the one to have the answers. She had become the leader of this motley group of castaways.

"Okay, so what does that mean, and what are we doing here in the dark?" She always had answers, but I always had one more question.

"It means we aren't safe. We're probably on their 'radar' now. And as soon as we can, we need to get out of here."

Tory broke in, "We can't go now, it's almost dark out there." The children tensed up, sensing the fear in her voice.

"You're right, but we can't just sit here." Mark earnestly replied.

"Over there, under the rug," Elle pointed to the far side of the large oval area rug some of us were sitting on, "is a trap door to a utility room, where the water heater, electric box, and furnace are. It might be a tight fit, but everyone can all squeeze down there, and if you're all silent as the dead... you just might stay alive."

"You said 'you' like **you** aren't joining us... or did I just read too much into that?" deciphered Mel.

"I'm not. Someone has to put the rug back and then draw them away from here. That someone is me."

"Elle, I'm not trying to sound sexist, but I can do this, you hide with everybody, and I will go." I was trying to do the right thing, besides, these people needed her... she had been the one who had kept them alive so far, and I didn't know if I, or anyone else here, could do that.

"No, I'm staying topside, and you have a bad leg anyway... that's like, not even fair, right?" She looked at me with sorrowful eyes, and I had a feeling that something, though I didn't know what was about to go terribly wrong.

"I don't have time to argue or explain right now, but Elle, you aren't staying up here alone. I'm staying with you." I smiled at her, thinking to myself that I was most likely committing suicide, but I was not about to hide in a hole while this incredible woman, once again, saved all of our hides.

She knew exactly what I was thinking, I could see the remorse on her face as she admitted, "I could use the backup... but everyone else, in the utility room now. No arguments!"

We rolled back the rug. Todd went first, followed by the children. Mel and his wife went next and then Mark and Darcy. Just as Tory was about to climb in, we heard a rustling noise off in the distance outside. Our widened eyes darted back and forth to each other, and Elle and I hurried Tory down the rabbit hole. I rolled the rug back into its place and Elle pointed to her ear twice and then to the door. I listened and she was right, the shuffling-rustling sounds were growing louder, closer. My heart sank and my stomach was in knots. They say you have butterflies in your stomach when you are nervous, but I had two rabid, fighting wolverines. I didn't know what to do, where to go, I was lost. I feared that busting out the front door would be like a scene from an old western...running out of a saloon with six-guns blazing, only to find ourselves in the midst of an ambush.

Fortunately, Elle grabbed my arm and pulled me with her to the back door. She drew back the corner of the curtain. Maybe the coast was clear, or maybe not, because she shoved a pistol in my hand, and drug over a backpack and pushed it to me. As I slid my arms into the straps and adjusted it on my shoulders, Elle slowly opened the door. I breathed a silent sigh of relief when it opened without a sound.

We were both hunkered down just inside the door that Elle held open with one hand. With the other hand, she reached over to me, placed her warm hand on the nape of my neck and pulled me to her. Her lips met mine in a flash of electricity and passion. As she pulled back from the kiss, my lower lip was caught as she sucked it between her lips, biting it gently and then broke the spell. "I just didn't want to have never done that... just in case," she whispered silently.

"Why didn't you just say it was for luck?" I winked back at her, though in this darkness, I wasn't sure if she could see my gesture. We slid silently from the back door, closing it as painstakingly as we had opened it. Like two untrained Navy Seals, we averted being seen by our predators, though we could hear the rustling of their purposeful strides not far behind us. Though we moved swiftly, we were overly careful, and I hoped we were, at least, moving swifter that the Takers behind us.

The sun had abandoned us, and the crescent sliver of a moon mocked us in the darkness of this unfamiliar territory as we climbed higher and higher into the mountainous terrain. When we came upon a washout, a place that appeared as if a giant had descended the beanstalk and scooped up a spoonful of the earth, we gathered ourselves within it. The hollowed area was only about eight feet across and three feet deep or so, but its rim was surrounded by the brush which gave us better cover.

The trees and sparse growth near the cabins had quickly evolved into a much denser forest as we had climbed, yet even in the arid darkness that surrounded us, we could see the geometric shapes of the cabins below. Through the protective cover of the surrounding brush, we studied the movement below.

"Look." Elle pointed towards the cabins, and though she didn't point to any one thing, in particular, I knew what she meant.

"I see them." It was a dizzying sight to behold as obvious clusters of the Takers meandered through the wooded area surrounding our last refuge, and the hiding place of the only other humans we knew in existence. I mean, seriously, we had no idea if these few Titans had accidentally crash landed here, or if it had been on purpose, much like we didn't know if there were others, in more populated places that had landed either. If Elle's tales had been accurate, I did understand more than a few things. Something like this would have immediately grabbed the attention of the NSA, and the government and military would have responded within minutes. It had been weeks. If they had attempted to respond, wouldn't Elle had experienced some kind of a fight? At least, there would have been explosions, gunfire, and fighter jets, maybe even stealth bombers trying to 'secure the area' as it was usually explained.

My heart sank to the depth that I felt nauseous when my stare fixed on one of the clusters entering the first cabin, followed by the second cabin being breached. I didn't close my eyes, but I did pray. I tucked the pistol into the waistband of my pants and slipped the pack off of my shoulders, setting it on the edge of our safe 'crater'.

"What do we do if they find the hiding place?" I couldn't help but ask.

"I wish I had all of the answers, but I don't," Elle grumbled in my ear.

"Well, what I'm asking is, do we hide and watch as they are taken and save ourselves, or do we go back and try to save them?" It was a stupid question, but I didn't want to be the one who answered it.

"We just do what we feel we have to do when we have to do it." It wasn't really an answer, but deep in my heart, I knew what she meant.

I looked over to see the silver of the crescent moon and starlight glimmering in her beautifully round eyes. Even in this moment of terror, and panic, I was falling for her. The memory of her kiss at the back door of the cabin was suddenly replaying in my mind, and I was glad there was darkness to hide the reddening of my face, as I felt the heat of my desire coming to the surface. I wanted to kiss her again, I wanted her, all of her. Though death knocked on our door, and newly made friendships may be meeting a horrifying demise... I wanted.

I was snapped back to reality with another hard, wet kiss and the sudden jerk of Elle's hand on my arm. "We gotta freakin' go!" It was far from a whisper and I felt confused until I saw them.

A whisper wouldn't have helped, not when there were six Takers somehow only a few short yards away.

We jumped from our hiding spots and bolted up the hillside. The adrenaline was overpowering my pain, and I was truly in a dead run, and still barely able to keep up with Elle. My heart pounded like it could explode from my chest at any moment, when Elle slipped, falling hard, face first to the ground. I stopped abruptly in my tracks to help her up and the earth itself seemed to be abuzz with our escape. I reached down and as I helped her up, I froze. Lights flickered above us and the ground buzzed again. Elle stood next to me, and I cradled her in my arms checking to see if she was alright. BOOM, the earth shook hard beneath us. Could it finally be the armed forces coming to save us, to save the planet? I thought in my comic book based thoughts. BOOM! The exploding sound thundered in the sky and shook the rocky earth beneath us. I looked up to see the lights, just like the night Elle had found me, scanning the mountaintop. BOOM! We fell as the ground shook so hard that the rocks and boulders broke free and tumbled aimlessly downward.

The lights swept down the mountainside and we couldn't keep ourselves from looking to see how close our pursuers had come when we were astonished to see that they had stopped their hunt for us and were retreating down the mountainside. As we looked on, BOOM, the methodical rhythm of the tremors became obvious, even to me. Elle pulled away and tried to pull me along with her, but I was caught in this surreal experience. I watched while the scanning lights grew brighter, and the scene surrounding the cabins became clear. The Takers were grouped in masses of three or four, each mass surrounding one of our friends. I felt not only helpless but hopeless. BOOM!!

Elle had no choice but to abandon me and pulled herself tight against the back wall of a washout, where earth and roots had formed an outcropping under which she had hidden from the approaching lights. It was then that I saw it for the first time. BOOM! The mass of the thing that impacted the ground was beyond anything my wildest imagination could have dreamed. I watched voiceless and incapable of movement as this Titan cleared the mountaintop perhaps a half mile from where we stood.

The front 'legs' of the Titans were considerably longer than the two in the rear. The massive body of the beast was unequaled to any moving thing I could have ever imagined. The possibilities of what it held within its metallic blue, geometric skin fluttered through my mind. Aside from frameworks and mechanics, there was most likely enough room to house an army or a prison...neither thought was comforting. Atop of the trapezoid body sat the headpiece. Similar to the turret of a tank without the barrel, it held one large 'eye' which shone like a spotlight into the emptiness of the desert night. Below its all-seeing eye was a series of seven much smaller red glowing lenses. Perhaps they were viewing points, or infrared lenses to see in the darkness that had not been illuminated by the light...or it could be some form of thermal imaging sensors, to pick up on the heat signatures of a generator, vehicle motor, or a life form, like myself.

I stood frozen in the blinding white of the ever-searching eye lights of the towering Titan. It halted less than 1000 yards from where I stood, hunkered over in its cyborg gorilla way, with its massive turret head swiveling side to side, sweeping the cliff walls and canyon floor for signs of life. With a thunderous boom and an earthshaking impact, the right front appendage moved forward. The movement mechanisms and pivoting points were filled with the blowing sand and had begun to rust causing the 'legs' of this mechanical giant to trill and groan as it moved in a stuttered way that only added to its eerie appearance.

The skin of the Titan was dark in color, but metallic and reflected the stars and the moon as it continued to pound away at the earth, trekking across a few miles in a short, dozen steps or so. As it passed the area that was once a serene and relaxing getaway where families would go to get away from the chaos of life and the horrors of everyday media, I realized that life, for me, would never, could never, be the same. I was sure that for those who survived this and still had their memories, it would leave them in post trauma.

I watched as the groups of Takers and our friends began trudging down the paved road to the flat desert area where the Titan had stopped. I began to feel that we had escaped a certain doom, if not death. I turned to find Elle still plastered up against the sandy dirt, tucked up under the outcropping. I reached out to her taking her hand. She opened her eyes and looking around stood up.

"We're alive," she said exuberantly, but no smile for me this time.

"Yes we are, but I can't say as much for our friends." I felt a guilt that was overwhelming.

"Oh, they are probably still alive, but they may not be our 'friends' for much longer. Soon they'll be Takers too."

"Awww, Elle... I'm sorry." I reached up to tuck her long hair behind her ear so I could see her beautiful face before I could complete my desire, my arm was jerked away from her, and she screamed. It was the loudest voice I could remember hearing. I was spun around like a toy and flung to the ground. It was a Taker! But where had he come from, and why hadn't he followed along with the others toward the Titan? He had tossed me aside like I was nothing to him. I felt like the geeky kid in school being pushed aside by the star football player, trying to get at the cheerleader, and I just happened to be in the way, like a piece of useless furniture. Elle's voice cut through me like a razor blade, deep and precise. My mind whirled with confusion, and I could only imagine her horror at the macabre reality before her.

She sobbed loudly, "OH Bobby... no-o-o!"

CHAPTER 5

UNINTENDED EVOLUTION

The Taker staggered closer reaching with open hands for Elle. She cowered, falling down on her butt, hands up in defense with her palms towards what was once her older brother, Bobby.

With a swift and muffled thud, the taker fell forward on top of her. She scrambled out from under him, as he lay lifeless face down in the sandy dirt. Elle peered up with tears streaming down her cheeks to see me standing over Bobby, still holding the blood stained rock in my hand. Nausea swept over me for a brief moment. This was the first life I had taken, and it probably would not be the last. I stepped to Elle, hoping to comfort her, and not become the monster who had just killed her brother when we both were stopped dead where we were. We were awestruck and bewildered as we watched an alien being separate itself from Bobby in a matter of seconds. The illuminated pale gray figure pulled its form directly from the still mass of the body that lay before us. It seemed fixated on Elle, and I couldn't have that.

In a few short steps, I burst forward and made my feeble attempt to slow or distract this thing. I was ready and willing to sacrifice myself to give Elle a running chance to save herself. I dove, wrapping my arms around its torso in a high school football style tackle. There was a jolt, like an electrical shock when you touch your tongue to a 9-volt battery, over the entirety of my body when I made contact. I slammed into the ground on top of it and much like it had been made of gelatin, I hit the ground hard as the form squished out from underneath me. It splattered and separated, and I found myself covered in the tingling, numbing "goo" that was the Ahsusha. I could not move, but watched and felt the entirety of its form quickly absorb into me, like water into a sponge until it could not be seen. The pain was like the uncomfortable pins and needles when one's leg falls asleep, not that slight tingling, but the intense feeling when the blood is rushing back to a limb that is completely asleep, dead weight, and you have to use another limb just to move it. Then suddenly everything went white and I imagined that this must be the feeling of being struck by lightning, or dying... or both.

Something inside of me caused my body to seize and convulse uncontrollably. As I spasmed, I threw myself onto my back, arching it in such an unnatural way that Elle was sure it would snap. She knew she should run, but after watching her brother attack her, and now seeing what appeared to be my obvious death, she felt helpless. It seemed pointless to run now.

Let the inevitable happen she thought, remembering how everyone she had tried to save over the past couple of weeks was surely experiencing what I was. She was the only one left, and the solitude was overwhelming.

She stared at my inhumanly arched position, my face inverted towards hers. My silent mouth opened wide, when suddenly my eyes shot open, and glared in her direction, with a faint green glow. My body collapsed and the Ahsusha poured out of me like my body had vomited it up from every pore. It had gathered into a formless massive blob, stretching tall and thin, and then falling over and back into itself repeatedly. Like a slinky made of gray jelly, it awkwardly retreated from us. Having stretched itself and moved fifteen feet away, or so, it stopped and lay there mostly still, except for a shuddering, pulsing, movement that slowed as the seconds past. Finally, it completely stopped and as it flattened out across the dirt and rocks like a melting popsicle, the dim gray luminosity faded from its being.

Elle's voice shook as she wept, "Please no, don't leave me all alone." I heard her plea and came to the realization that I was not, in fact, dead, which pleased me.

Every muscle and every inch of my body ached. This must be the feeling of being tasered...repeatedly, I thought. Struggling to regain control of my body, I attempted to roll onto my side and get up, a task that proved to be impossible at this point, but I did manage to roll onto my side and raise my upper body up, supporting myself under my wobbly arms. My movements were slow and unnatural, and my eyesight was still a bit blurred.

Everything had gone white, but now it was slowly starting to dim, though it was pitch black outside, it felt like driving west as the sun was going down. I could see, but I couldn't focus well because of the blindingly bright glare.

I squinted up at Elle, thrilled and amazed that we were still alive when suddenly she screamed like a banshee and thrust herself on top of me in a fit of rage. Straddling my midsection, she began pummeling my head and chest with her fists, not as if she thought she would beat me to death, but in anger and frustration, almost as if she were provoking a fight. I pained myself to squeak out a few words from my dried throat.

"Elle, please..." I tried to swallow. Her fists hammered my head so hard it literally bounced off of the ground. "Elle, don't kill me...I..I'm sorry."

Elle stopped instinctively when she heard the words and stood up, stammering backward. "You... you're alive? For real?" she quizzed me, sounding more puzzled with each word that escaped her lips. She wiped the sweat from her forehead and chin and stepped back so she could catch herself and lean against the outcropping.

"Yeah...I'm alive." I collected myself and found myself more confused with each passing moment. "What happened here?" I said looking around, but before she could answer I blurted out, "Oh My God Who is that? Is he alright?"

"That's my brother....Bobby!" she spoke with obvious anger and frustration in her voice as she over-emphasized his name. "Alright? I doubt it! What's wrong with you, you freak!?!?"

"I don't know what's wrong with me. I hurt all over, and I can't see right." I paused afraid to admit to Elle, and to myself, the whole truth. "How did we get here? And... please, please, please don't take this wrong..." my voice was as weak as I was, but I pleaded as best as I could, "how do we know each other? I mean, I know you... you are Elle, right?" I was sadly lost.

"Um, yeah... remember when we ran up here from the cabin to get away from the takers?...that's how we got here." I couldn't tell if there was more frustration or concern in Elle's voice now.

"Wow... I'm kinda woozy feelin'... can we go back to that cabin you were talkin' about and maybe just lay down for a while... I don't feel so good." I drew a deep breath. "I feel...wrong."

"Aw, hell!" Elle muttered. I think we had better stay here for now. That Titan isn't far enough away for me to feel comfortable taking you back down there right now...besides, I need to do something with Bobby. I can't just leave my own brother lying dead, face down like that." Elle had decided that when it was safe to move, we would take Bobby back down near the cabin, try to find a shovel or something to dig with, and bury him...maybe, she thought, she would even say a prayer or something, though she wasn't particularly religious, and the arrival of the Ahsusha had shaken what little faith she did have.

For the time being, Elle decided to roll him over on his back. Face down seemed to remove all dignity from the thing laying there that she once called family. When she had done that, she scooted his legs together in a normal position and folded his hands across his chest. The last thing she chose to do was to ask me to remove my shirt to cover his face.

She sat down a few feet from where her brother laid, and invited me to sit with her. The air was growing quite cool on my bare upper body. Elle sat there staring off into the dark nothingness of the night, listening to the far-off hum and occasional vibrato of the Titan's movements. It did seem to be moving away from us, which, I guessed accurately, was a good thing. Her hair was a tasseled mess, the sundress was dirt stained and torn, and Elle reminded me of an orphan child from a third world 'help the starving and homeless for only $0.37 a day' advertisement. She looked broken, and I reached my arm out and gathered her into me, wrapping my arm around her shoulder and combing my fingers through her hair. She closed her eyes to forget the tragedies of the day and take a brief moment to enjoy. We became momentarily lost in the now.

Taking comfort in the idea that, for all practical purposes, we were alone, we melted into each other and just existed for a while. Though I couldn't really remember how I knew Elle, it just felt right. The thought crossed my mind that perhaps we were related, but I reasoned that away instantly. If that had been the case, she wouldn't have told me that Bobby was her brother. Were we married? I caressed her shoulder with my left hand as a distraction so she wouldn't notice that I was rubbing my fingers together to feel for a wedding band. There wasn't one. Were we dating, engaged, lifelong friends... I didn't know the answer, but at this moment, I didn't care to know. In my mind, at this point in the fabric of time, however, brief it may be, she was my everything.

Nearly half an hour had passed while we enjoyed the intimacy and solitude of the mountain side, with the tremors and electrical humming of the Titan growing ever farther from our ears and our minds. Though I still didn't know my role in Elle's life, I had come to a decision. I was going to kiss her. My left arm and hand had been around her back, gently rubbing and caressing her shoulder and arm. I nervously slid my hand from her shoulder to her neck, and then beyond to the long tangles of her ebony hair. I clenched my fingers together almost making a fist, pulling her hair and causing her to react by arching her neck back, exposing it and her full, pouty lips to me. I leaned into her, and softly brushed my lips against the tanned skin of her neck, exhaling my hot breath slowly as I kissed my way up across her cheek. Her moans were nearly silent, but they existed, none the less, which gave me courage. I kissed again, and again she sighed, until ultimately, I reached the cherry redness of her lips. Their softness was only matched by her willingness and obvious desire and enjoyment. Our hands searched each other's bodies as our kisses became more passionate, our tongues connecting with the excitement, like the spark of electricity.

Our mouths broke free from their bond long enough to draw in a deep breath and gaze into each other's eyes. Elle gasped out loud and scurried backward until she had collided with the body of her brother who had lain there, silently, almost forgotten in the throes of passion. But, his silence too, was broken. He groaned ever so lightly, and Elle once again nearly jumped out of her skin.

"Oh fuck! Oh fuck!" she jumped up grabbing handfuls of her own hair as she paced a quick three step-turn-three step pace. "Holy fucking crap!"

"What do we do? He isn't dead!!!" I pointed out the obvious.

"But you.." she stammered, "Your eyes," she spoke quietly, raising her hand to her mouth, as if in disbelief. "Can you see me? Are you okay?"

"I'm fine," though that was really far from the truth, "My vision is kinda screwed up, to be honest, but I can see you... prolly better that if it was normal. It's prolly pretty dark out here, *isn't it?*"

Elle seemed frightened. "You sure you are okay?" She asked again but kept her distance. Bobby began to take audible breaths, and it was a much-needed distraction.

"I'm fine." I reiterated. "Now...what are we going to do with.." I gestured towards Bobby. I didn't know what to call him... a him, it, a taker, Bobby... I didn't want to offend her by de-humanizing him, and I did not want to give her false hope by making her think of him as her brother. If we had to 'put him down' I would rather she thought of him as a 'zombie-Taker' than as her own brother.

"Maybe it's safe enough to head back down to the cabin. If he doesn't wake up, maybe we can carry him down there and tie him up until he does come around." She rubbed her forehead and I knew she was more thinking out loud, than telling me her plans. "What do you think?"

"Well, I know those things are pretty damn strong, right?" She nodded in response. "So, what if we do get him there and tie him up... he may just break free, or worse. I mean, Hell, he could come to while we are carrying him down there."

"Okay..points made and taken, but we can't just leave him here.. not just because he is my brother, but because he is a Taker. That could be more dangerous than bringing him with us. He could come back with a whole army of those things."

It was comforting in a creepy sort of way to hear her call them 'things'. It eased my tensions about her not being able to break the sibling bond should the Taker wake up and not be any more 'Bobby" than when I struck him with the stone I had picked up.

"Alright.. you have made your point too. We will carry him to the cabin, if we can, and then do our best to restrain him. You do realize that that means we will have to take turns watching him. We won't be able to both rest at the same time."

"I'm cool with that." she said nonchalantly.

"K.. then we better get going." I was unsure of our decision, but I didn't feel we had time to safely consider all of our limited options in depth.

"Right. He could wake up anytime." She concurred.

"I'll take the head, you take the feet." I said, not trying to take command of the situation, but because I knew the bulk of the dead weight would be at the upper half of the body. I squatted down at his head, and carefully slid my arms under his and around his chest. Elle reached down and took one ankle in each had and with nods of agreement, we stood up.

"Well Hell! Put him back down easy." I said, and Elle scrunched her eyebrows at me in confusion. "I got this. He doesn't weigh anything."

Once he was laid down again, I stood to face him and grabbed him up by the waist. As gently as I could, I placed him on my shoulder and holding him in place with one hand, I slightly bowed and gracefully extended my other arm. "After you m'lady." I jested with a smile.

I followed Elle back down the path we had taken when we fled the invasion of the Takers only a few hours ago. At first, I thought she was checking on me to make sure I was okay and was keeping up with her, but I began to realize that there was a concern in her eyes when she would look over her should to me. And the farther we went, the more frequently she would look. If she was wondering if I was getting tired of carrying Bobby, she needn't worry; carrying him was no more difficult than packing a sack of potatoes on my shoulder.

After what felt like a short hike (possibly because we were going downhill this time) we arrived back at the cabins. This place seemed familiar, but everything in my memory was still such a blur. With each passing minute, the fog was becoming less and less dense in my mind.

The front door stood wide open, and through the darkness, I could easily see the interior was in a state of disarray. I carried Bobby to one of the bedrooms and laid him on his back on the bed. Elle nervously lit two candles. She sat one on the nightstand and took one with her to look for anything to tie up her brother with. I stood guard over him like a silent sentinel, awaiting any movement, no matter how slight.

Elle quickly searched the house and the cellar utility room for something to restrain him. She immediately found a sheet that could be cut into strips to tie his hands and feet, but she did not stop. Elle understood the strength that the Takers had, and ripped cotton cloths would not hold him. After finishing on the main level, she crept down into the utility room. Searching and scouring the boxes and shelves, she came across screws and nails, tape and scissors. There were bits of wrapping paper, extension cords and pictures framed for hanging that were so atrocious they didn't even deserve to be in a cellar. 'Wait', Elle thought to herself, 'extension cords'. She turned back to the box that held the cords and ransacked her way through it, digging out three heavy duty cords of various lengths. Snatching up the scissors on her way out of the cellar, she quietly and swiftly entered the bedroom.

Elle unwound the first cord. It appeared to be around twenty feet in length. Straightening it out and folding it in half, Elle withdrew the scissors from the pocket on the front of her sundress and began the strenuous task of trying to cut through it. Her hand was growing tired and pained as she sawed the scissors open and closed across the cord. The thumb and finger holes of the scissors rubbed reddened circles until finally, she had to stop.

"Damn it." she muttered, stretching her hand and massaging the reddened areas.

"Let me try for a minute while you give your hand a rest." I smiled at her, but she stared blankly into my eyes. I hoped my intuition was wrong, but somehow, I sensed fear in her as I took the scissors and cord from her. I poised the edges of the scissors into the underwhelming cuts Elle had already begun. With a bit of force, I made my first attempt and cut the cord into two pieces like I was cutting through a piece of shoestring licorice.

I shrugged my shoulders and raised my eyebrows with a half-smile. Handing her back the scissors, I reassured her. "You must have gotten through the tough part before I took over."

Unraveling the other two shorter cords, we gently tied Bobby by his wrists and ankles to the thick timbers of the rustic four poster bed. When we had finished, I felt comfortable in the security of his bindings. Tight enough that he could not slip out, but not so much that it could cut off his circulation. He looked odd laying there motionless in his tattered clothing, spread eagle on the bed. My hopes of sleeping in this bed had been thrown out the window, but there was another bed, and since we wouldn't be sleeping simultaneously, it would do just fine.

"I'm gonna grab a washcloth and a bowl of water. Be right back." Elle left me alone with her brother again, and I couldn't stop my mind from wondering, why had the woman who had been so flirty, and even kissed me earlier, now felt uncomfortable around me.

She returned and cut straight to the bedside, shooting me a sideways look of distrust. I was lost. The memories were all coming back quite clearly now, at least as far back as my being alone in the desert, and as hard as I tried, I couldn't recall anything I had done, or said, that would have caused her to flip on the 'cold shoulder' switch so abruptly.

Elle sat on the bed next to her brother, placing the bowl on the nightstand next to the candle, and dampened the washcloth in the water. His hair was a matted mess of dirt and sand, and wet and dried blood. She began to blot and rub the bloodied mess and clean away the gritty, reddish brown blood from his forehead and face.

"That looks refreshing. If you are okay, I'm gonna go splash some water on my face."

"Go ahead. I'm fine." Her words were cold and flat.

I grabbed up one of the candles and took it with me to the bathroom. Placing it on the top of the toilet tank I reached over and turned on the faucet. The water was cold and crisp, and though it was a shock to the system, it was an awakening I needed. I snatched a hand towel to dry my face and looked up to give myself a look of displeasure. I wasn't sure who I was in my previous 'real world' life, but I was fairly certain that I was no lady killer. I was also pretty sure that I hadn't done anything that would have so blatantly repulsed Elle.

Suddenly, there it was. "Dear God!" I said directly out loud. I stared into my own eyes, not even recognizing my own reflection. There, in the mirror, were two eyes, slightly luminous, pupils... pale green, and whites that were only slightly bloodshot. What the hell? The Ahsusha had attacked me, I remember that now, but what had happened to it, and what the hell had happened to me. I began to think about the events that I had thought nothing about, but now I began to question a few things. I reached down and peeled back the bandages on my calf. The wound was all but healed. Somehow, I had carried a full grown man down the hillside without even giving my leg a thought, when just before the attack, I had struggled to climb the hill, hobbling on my leg that was nearly disabling.

My mind was working overtime, working better that it ever had, better than it should, and it started explaining itself to me. It began to make sense of things I couldn't and I found my thoughts explaining **everything** to me. I wondered if this was how a schizophrenic felt. It felt like there were almost two consciousnesses inside my head. I understood that when I was overtaken by the Ahsusha it should have drained the life energy from me starting in my brain where a vital energy exists. I should have become one of the Takers, controlled by the Ahsusha who had taken me, that is unless it had not stopped, in which case I would have been drained of every bit of life force. In the case of the latter, I would have been used up and dropped like a deflated balloon: limp, lifeless, dead.

Instead, when I was attacked, something had sort of repulsed that beast, and it had retreated and quickly met its own demise, but that wasn't all. I had gained some things from its possession of me. I was notably stronger than I had been, my leg had healed almost entirely in a matter of minutes, and though my eyes had the frightening look of an undead alien, I could now see quite well in the darkness. I wondered if there would be more that had changed, things I hadn't discovered yet. Would there be things about me that would continue to evolve? I hadn't asked for this, and I certainly didn't want it. I should have been dead, or a mindless slave like the others. Either of those might have been better, or, at least, easier to deal with than being forced to accept that I was evolving into something that was no longer 100% human. I didn't know if there were pieces of my humanity that were gone and had been replaced by attributes that were alien to me; things that were simply alien.

CHAPTER 6

FAMILIAR STRANGER

I have no idea how long I stood there leaning on the sink edge, staring blankly at the stranger in the mirror before I gathered myself. "What the Hell is going on?" I muttered to myself. Fear let in a multitude of improbabilities, including the possibility that this thing that attacked me hadn't died, and perhaps I hadn't won. Had I become a host to some alien race and would soon become some zombified 'Taker' like so many others I had seen? Sweat beaded heavy and cold on my brow and my stomach turned and knotted as the thought of changing into some mindless slave that would turn on my new found friends. I had to talk to Elle about the chance that I could become the enemy. An insurmountable wave of anxiety washed over me making it difficult to breathe or even focus on anything but the fear that I could soon die at the hands of a woman I might be falling in love with. Love... a strong word, but this woman was beyond amazing. Elle had single-handedly saved me and countless others, putting her own life on the line for a hodge-podge of complete strangers. She had selflessly tried to help every single person she had encountered, and every person she had encountered was now dead... except for me and her brother, but my intuition told me this could and probably would change all too soon.

I splashed my face with a bit more icy water to rinse the beads of sweat from my face and patted it dry once again. A knock came at the door just as I hung the towel in its place on the rack.

"You okay in there?" The soft voice of Elle filled the silent space.

"Yeah, I guess. I'll be right out." I wasn't really okay. I felt slightly nauseous thinking of an inevitable conversation we would soon be having.

"Okay... Just checking." There was a compassion in her tone that I hadn't expected. Though a part of her instinctively feared me like a monster from a black and white horror film, there was another part that she kept hidden deep within herself that genuinely cared. It could be that she felt sorry for me and related my situation to her brother's and to all of the Takers that she had put down.

I turned to grab the candle when I realized it had completely burned down and left an eerie, waxy mess on the back of the toilet. Not only had I been staring in the mirror far longer than I realized, but the flame had gone out and I hadn't even noticed. I had wasted a candle that Elle could have used, and we couldn't just 'run to the dollar store' to get another. I grabbed the doorknob, drew a deep breath and gave it a twist. Another thing I hadn't noticed until I opened the door was that the length of time I had spent in the tiny bathroom caused the air to grow close and stuffy. The cooler air rushed in from the hallway and felt so refreshing I nearly sighed out loud. I meandered back into the bedroom where Elle's brother Bobby was confined to the bed. Elle had finally relaxed a bit and melted against the wall near the head of the bed.

"I'm sorry I was kind of harsh, but..." She tried, awkwardly, and failed to make eye contact with me.

"Stop... just stop." I studied the lines in the hardwood floorboards and swayed timidly. "I didn't know... not until I looked in the mirror. I guess I'd be pretty freaked out too if I was you. Looking back, I'm really surprised you didn't shoot me at first sight."

She smiled kindly but never raised her eyes. "I can't say it hasn't crossed my mind... a couple of times."

"Yeah." I stumbled with my words, but in my mind, I knew it was probably the best time to spill my thoughts. "You might have to..." My voice cracked and then trailed off. "...at some point."

"Come on! I was just kidding." She finally looked up and mumbled "Sort of..." When her eyes met mine, I could sense that she could read the sorrow and despair I was feeling and that perhaps there was some honesty and seriousness to my words.

"There's something going on in my head, and probably all of me, that I don't understand. That thing attacked me, but it 'died' or whatever." I rubbed my fingers across the stubbly 5 o'clock shadow on my jawline. "It may have died, but something has happened to me too. I don't have to tell you that."

"True..." She began. "...but you're still alive, can still talk and think straight, so...I don't know what happened to you."

"That's just it. I don't know either. There are crazy things happening and thoughts running through my brain. I thought I won that fight, but I'm starting to wonder if I have some sort of alien parasite or something. Maybe I'll still turn into one of those Taker things." I ran my hands through my hair and rubbed my face vigorously as if I would somehow snap back to normal, but I knew that I wouldn't. "So, if I am still fighting a battle on the inside, and I lose... you have to do what you have to do to stay alive."

"I'll stay alive. I am strong and fast. I will outrun you and get away." She tried to avoid the reality of it all. "No need to talk about all this 'you might still have to shoot me' stuff."

"I want you to make me a promise." I knelt down in front of her, took her chin in my hand and raised it up until her eyes met mine. I looked past the dark brown beauty of them and right into her soul and could feel her tremble in acknowledgment.

"Okay... ?" She agreed with a questioning tone.

"If it ever gets to the point of no return... if the time comes that I'm no longer human... no longer me, don't leave me like that.

Put me down. I don't want to hurt anyone, and I sure as hell don't want to live like that." My eyes welled up and the emotion ran down my cheeks as I drew the pistol from my waistband and laid it in her lap. "Deal?" I squeaked out in a whisper.

"Deal." She lipped the word silently as she realized deep down I was the same man she had desired not such a long time ago.

She leaned forward, closing her eyes to hide her own tears and pressed her lips softly against mine, with a gentle kiss. I slipped my hand onto the nape of her neck as I took her lower lip between mine and then released it, making the slightest smacking sound. The adrenaline flowed and I could sense the synchronicity of our hearts as they raced. My face grew flushed as I pulled her closer and pressed my open mouth against her neck just below her ear, kissing it ever so slowly and exhaling loudly before kissing it again. Her voice moaned soft and heavenly when I took her earlobe between my lips and nibbled at it tenderly. Our breathing was heavy, and the sweat of our bodies was not simply the lack of air conditioning in this sultry cabin. We were creating something from nothing... passion was the magic we had manifested from thin air and it was now so heavy, it was nearly unbearable.

There was another moan and groan that shook us from our self-created nirvana and back into the horrific reality of life. Bobby was stirring, and it shook us back to the dread we had so briefly escaped as fast as waking up by being doused with a bucket of ice water.

"Bobby!" She called out, jumping to her feet. "Bobby, can you hear me?" His body stirred slightly, still bound to the sturdy bedposts as if in preparation for some medieval torture. Elle tucked the pistol between the mattress and box springs without ever taking her eyes from her brother.

"Here." I wrung out the washcloth and handed it to her.

"Bobby, it's me, Elle. Can you hear me, Bobby?" She hunkered down over him and whispered as she dabbed the cool, damp cloth on his cheeks and forehead. He groaned again and it was obvious that he was extremely weak and incoherent.

"Do you want me to get a fresh washcloth and water?" I asked.

"Please?" She responded with compassion. "Not too much. It's hard to say how much water pressure we will have without the generator to run the well pump."

"Oh!" My eyes widened. "I hadn't thought about that."

"That's whatcha got me for." She genuinely smiled and winked at me. "I grew up in the sticks. Anytime the power went out, I remember my parents worried about losing water pressure."

I disappeared into the hallway and quickly returned with a fresh washcloth and the bowl half full with fresh, cool water. I placed it gingerly on the floor beside Elle and knelt down beside her. She turned her back to me, bent over, and laid the washcloth that was stained pinkish-tan from the blood and dirt on the floor and dunked the new one into the bowl. I heard her suck her breath in when her hand met the chilly water. Elle remained standing but turned back toward her resting brother. While she wiped his face and neck with the fresh cloth, she paused and looked over her shoulder to where I was.

"Sorry. I probably just put my butt right in your face, didn't I?" She raised her eyebrows and rolled her eyes.

"Maybe... I didn't really notice." I winked. "probably should do it again, and I'll let you know."

Elle smiled and her face reddened. "If you're lucky," She whispered, wiggled her hips and then turned her attention back to her brother, who had quieted down.

I watched her silently as she tended to what could be her only family. Eventually, she knelt down with her butt on her heels and submerged the washcloth in the water bowl. I wrapped my arm around her shoulder and gave her a squeeze.

"No matter what happens, it's going to be alright," I spoke softly into her ear.

"How can you believe that?" She turned and frowned at me. "Nothing is alright. My whole damn world is falling apart, and in case you haven't looked in the mirror lately, so is yours." Her voice was stern.

"Yeah..." I muttered under my breath and could feel my whole body lose   its last shred of hope, but something I couldn't explain told me it wasn't as bad as it all seemed.

"I'm sorry." Her gaze dropped to the floor. "It's just... well, I've seen what happens to people, and I've seen what it did to Bobby... and all of those people that we abandoned here that were taken, what about them? How can I believe that any of them are going to be alright?" Her hand stretched out and took hold of mine. "Right now, to me, you are the only person in the world, and..." Elle inhaled deeply and let out a quiet sigh. "I don't think I could take losing you too."

It was at that very moment that the unthinkable happened. Another moan from the lips of Elle's brother Bobby quickly stole our attention away from our moment of personal struggles and vulnerability. Bobby stirred and actually made a poor attempt to struggle against the wire bonds. He was intentionally moving and perhaps waking, and I knew this could go very badly. I mentally prepared and expected the worst. I did not want to have to fight and possibly kill Elle's brother right in front of her. There is no way that we would ever be able to look at each other the same if that happened.

"If he comes to and breaks loose, I want you to get out of here as quick as you can. Let me handle him." I spoke in a normal volume, yet remained monotone so as to not stir up her emotions any more than they already were. "If this goes badly, I don't want you to be here."

"I don't know if I can..." Her words were cut short and we were both dumbfounded.

"Elle... is that you?" A dry and raspy voice struggled with the words.

"Bobby! Is that really you?" Elle dropped to her knees at his side and the emotions were so overpowering that tears flowed and she began to sniffle immediately.

"It's me sis, but not for long." Elle feared what he meant, but there were two definite possibilities. Neither of them was good.

I could see that speaking pained him terribly and I rushed to the kitchen for a glass of water. I scurried to grab a plastic cup from the cabinet and fill it with water. The pressure was dwindling and I stopped at half a cup in case there was some emergency call for water that I couldn't anticipate. I returned only moments later to find Elle having untied one of his wrists, clutching his hand and weeping. I feared the worst, but his head rolled to the side and his eyes opened with a dim inhuman glow. I handed the cup to Elle and slid my hand under his head and raised it slightly. She pressed the rim of the plastic cup to his lips and he graciously took the smallest of sips before turning away.

His eyes were fixed on Elle as he spoke. "I'm not human anymore..." A labored breath was drawn and though he couldn't even find the strength to move his head, he turned his eyes to me. "...neither are you, my brother."

"Yes, you are," Elle reassured him. "You know me. You've come back to me."

"No, I'm both... we're both." He batted his watering eyes open and closed and a single tear rolled out of the corner of his eyes and down the sides of his face to his ears. "I..." He paused to take a short awkward breathe and his eyelids fluttered wildly. When they stopped, and he slowly opened them once again, the glow began to dim and die, revealing dark brown irises. "I came back to say goodbye."

"No, you can't do that. I thought I lost you once already. Don't make me lose you again." Elle sniffled uncontrollably, but her words were too late.

I could feel Bobby's body relax in my hand and we heard that unmistakably putrid sound of the 'death rattle' as his last breath escaped his body and left an empty envelope that once held a life that was so precious to Elle. For me, it was a moment of immeasurable sorrow and anxiety. Elle was all that I had in this world, and now, I was all that she had. What if this was what would inevitably happen to me too? My mind was a blur with mixed up thoughts and emotions and I almost forgot where I was and that I still held Bobby's lifeless head in my hand. The realization brought me back to reality, a very twisted and surreal reality, but reality none the less. I laid his head gently on the pillow, and placed my hands on Elle's shoulders as she sobbed at his side.

I stood behind where she knelt for what felt like hours. When Elle had finally run out of tears, she released Bobby's hand and slowly pulled her trembling body to its feet. I placed my chin on her shoulder and whispered into her ear.

"I am so sorry Elle." I was at a loss for words, and though I knew she would have a very valid argument to my statement, I said it anyway. "I will not leave you."

She turned her face toward mine and gently kissed my cheek. "Never..." She whispered. "...and I will never leave you." She turned to me and we embraced, just holding each other close and comforting one another silently.

***

The dawn would come quickly, which was apparently a good thing. There was an unmistakable feeling that we needed to move on when the sun broke the horizon and I knew we needed to act quickly so that we could get as much distance behind us as possible while the daylight allowed, but there were other things to consider, and other things to do before we headed out to

"We need to go as soon as the sun is up, right?" I asked what felt like an obvious question.

"Yes we should, but we can't just leave him here like this." Elle glared off into space, deep in thought and memories. "Can we bury him?"

"That would take some time. What about a stone grave? We could wrap him in soft blankets and place him somewhere and cover him with a mound of stones." I had seen this somewhere, but I had no idea where.

"Okay. That seems fitting." She replied, her voice devoid of emotion. "Where?"

"I remember seeing a lot of boulders and large stones on the hill near the dug out spot where we first saw him." I offered a suggestion.

"Yes." She nodded. "That is where he should be laid to rest, where we saw him and where you overtook him. That is what eventually gave us a chance to say goodbye."

Elle chose several soft and quilted blankets from a linen closet and layered them on the floor. On the top, she placed a thick sub-zero, arctic sleeping bag. I took great care in picking up Bobby, but I was not prepared for the wave of sorrow that overtook me as I carried the man who was for all intents and purposes a complete stranger. I related to him as a threat for the entire time I had 'known' him with the exception of the last hour of his life. There was a dark and demented comfort in knowing that part of me was still human; part of me had to be to feel such confusing emotions. I laid him out on the unzipped sleeping bag, and straightened his legs, and crossed his arms. Elle zipped up the arctic bag and pulled the drawstring tight, closing the opening where his face was. We began to wrap the blankets around him until the last blanket, which was a deep forest green, was finally in place.

CHAPTER 7

MOVING DAY

It was a long and arduous journey to lay brother Bobby in his final resting place. The trip back down to the cabins found us numb and silent. We stood in the darkness at the back of the cabin and I waited for Elle to speak. She took a step back and shook with a chill.

"I can't go back in there," She whispered so quietly I thought she must know something I didn't.

"What is it? Did you see something, or hear something?" I asked.

"No. It's just that all I would be able to think of is Bobby." Her head lowered. "I'm just not ready."

"Oh, of course!" I felt like an idiot. "Let's go to the other cabin and get some rest. We're going to need it if we are going to be hiking all day tomorrow."

I wrapped my arm around her waist and led her to the twin cabin just a few short steps away. We made our way inside and I had forgotten that she could not see as well as I could in the pitch black of the interior. She misstepped and ran into an end table in the front room, flinching and groaning in pain. I reached into my pocket and drew out a red disposable lighter that Elle had given me after lighting the candles earlier. The flint wheel spun under the pressure of my thumb and the flame appeared lighting the area only slightly.

"Have a seat and I'll go find a candle." I motioned to the empty couch near where she stood.

Her body seemed to sink into the plaid, overstuffed cushions and with a few fluttering blinks, her eyes closed. I took my thumb off of the lever and let the lighter go out. My newly acquired ability to see fairly well in the dark was more helpful than I would have ever imagined. I had only briefly been inside this cabin, and I was surprised to find it was completely different than the other, which made my search take a little longer than I had expected. I was pleasantly surprised when I opened up the hallway closet to not only find a box of emergency candles but two lanterns and a full gallon can of fuel. I took one of the candles to the kitchen and took a saucer from the cabinet. When the candle was lit, I turned it on its side and let the wax drip onto the plate and then pressed the base of the candle into the soft puddle. I cupped my hand around it and walked back into the front room.

Elle was curled up on the couch and sound asleep from exhaustion. I smiled, blew out the candle and sat down gently on the recliner. I rested with one eye open until the sun began to lighten the dusty curtains. It was just about then that I dozed off. I did not dream, I did not toss and turn. Truthfully, I don't think I moved even a fraction of an inch until I was startled awake by a clattering racket from the kitchen. The sun was blazing high in the sky and almost pained my eyes when I leapt to my feet. Confused and disoriented I sped into the eat-in-kitchen, just a few long strides away. I found Elle on the floor half inside of one of the cabinets and an array of items from canned goods to Tupperware covering the counter tops, table, and floor.

"What's going on?" I said surprised by what I had found.

A loud 'thud' was followed by a long string of cuss words. She backed out of the cabinet rubbing her head with one hand and awkwardly holding a large box of cereal in the other. "Damn that hurt."

"Sorry. I didn't mean to startle you, but seriously, why didn't you wake me up?" It was an emotional tug of war. I was upset with myself for causing her to hit her head, there was a feeling of remorse and sorrow for Elle's lost brother, but above all, right at this moment, I was angry that she had left me asleep while the sun was making it way across the sky all too quickly.

"Well... I didn't know how long you were asleep." She tried to play the 'thoughtful card' but I wasn't sure I was buying into it. "Besides..." She said as she began to stick her nose into the next cabinet. "...I just got up a few minutes ago."

"And you made all this mess in a few minutes?" I shot her a look of disbelief.

"No, of course not." She popped her head out of the cabinet and shook an unopened bag of corn chips at me. "Bingo! Score!" She pumped her fist in the air. "All this mess took over a week to make. I didn't know if there was anything left to eat here, but look at everything I found!"

Elle seemed pleased with her progress and genuinely smiled, catching me completely off guard. I knew she wasn't being honest. I had been in the kitchen just a few hours earlier, and this mess did not exist then. All the same, I said nothing and let her continue in her search and pleasant mood. I expected days or even weeks of depression. Perhaps this was just a mood swing and wouldn't last, or maybe she was in denial... on the other hand, she had watched as three massive alien structures crashed into the desert, glowing alien blob-things had been sucking the life out of people and turning them into alien-zombies right before her eyes (including her brother) and had lost everyone she had saved except for me... maybe this was genuine and she was a 'take each moment as it comes' kind of girl. One thing was certain: in the daylight, with that smile... her eyes were the most beautiful thing I believed I had ever seen.

"I guess we had better get packed up and moving pretty damn quick if we're going to put any miles behind us before dusk." I urged her on though I didn't want to spoil this moment.

"About that... um, no." Elle had caught me completely off guard.

"What do you mean... 'um no', seriously?" I knew we couldn't stay here. We might last a week before the food ran out, and that's only if those things didn't come back sooner.

"I mean, I think we slept longer than you realize... by the time we get everything packed it's going to be close to dark. We have to stay here one more night. It has to be safer than traveling at night." She sat down on the kitchen floor and crossed her legs, grabbing the box of whole grain cereal, opening it and grabbing a handful to munch on.

"Okay then... where do we start?" I leaned over and as I kissed her forehead, I stole a handful of cereal for myself.

"Gotta find some backpacks, bags, anything we can cram full of whatever we might need." She made a good point. We needed to know how much we had room for before we decided what to take.

"Oh, hey... we'd better find everything we can find to carry water in, too. No telling when we will come across drinkable water again, or any water." I started to look around at the Tupperware and wondered what else we might find. "Okay, I'll tell you what...

I'm going next door and I'll rummage through and see what I can find and when I get it all together, I'll come help you."

"Then we'll start up the generator, get the water pump going and maybe even run the air conditioner for a bit." She stood up and gave me a quick hug.

"Sounds like a plan," I said as I hugged her back.

After a moment of awkward silence, I turned and left the room, and then the cabin. Elle had been right. From the sun's place in the sky, I could tell it was well past noon, and the day had heated up to what felt like 110 degrees. I searched the surrounding area for any movement or sounds from the porch of the cabin, but silence filled my ears, an eerie, empty silence. It felt uncomfortable being outside alone and I hastily crossed the empty space between the vacation cabins. With one last glance over my shoulder, I threw the front door open and rushed inside, closing the door quickly behind me. Much like Elle had been when we had come down the hill in the dark, I felt like something wasn't right, like perhaps I wasn't alone. I began searching the hall closet first, and then room by room, I gathered whatever I thought might be of any help. I packed all of the items into the living room and arranged them by category and most to least valuable for survival: weapons, carry bags, medicines, food, toiletries, clothes, etc...

It took nearly an hour and a half to go through the small two bedroom cabin, and when I was about to start packing it over to where Elle was, I had a flash of memory. Under the rug... there was a trap door to the cellar and mechanical room under the living room rug. There could certainly be some useful tools or weapons stored there. I grabbed the edge of the rug, pulled it back on top of itself and froze when I swore there was a faint sound, like something shuffling beneath the floor boards. I panicked and threw the rug back over the trap door and pulled a recliner over the top.

A sudden 'tap-tap-tap-, click-creeeeak' series of sounds came from behind me and I spun about and sprung towards the door with the speed and stealth of a cheetah. I landed squarely on top of the intruder, hands around their neck, and nearly made short work of the only other human being I knew.

"What the hell!" Elle exclaimed.

"I'm... I'm so sorry." I loosened my grip and scrambled backward. "You startled me." It was then I remembered the sound that I thought came from the cellar. I decided not to mention the sound from under the floor, mostly because I was beginning to believe the sound may have been Elle leaving the cabin next door.

"Um, okay." She brushed herself off and regained her composure. "Guess I don't have to worry about anyone getting the jump on us."

I apologized, at least, four more times while Elle and I began to dig through my finds and sorting out the 'must haves' from the 'wants'. We began packing a backpack full of canned goods, a couple of knives, forks and spoons, a can opener, a roll of aluminum foil, and two small plastic cups.

"Can't forget these." Elle finally broke a smile as she neatly tucked a picnic set of salt and pepper shakers into the quickly filling pack.

"Those are necessities?" I was puzzled.

"You will be glad we have them after a week of eating dry cereal and canned goods." She smiled again, knowing it was a choice of desire, not need, and I could not argue with that smile.

The pack was topped off with a flat sheet filled with all of the bandages, meds, and toiletries that would fit. Holes were poked in the corners of two pillows and they were clipped onto a carabiner on the outside of it. An assortment of knives, a hammer, and two boxes of .22 caliber shells were wrapped in two blankets and stuffed into the duffel bag. I added a few pairs of pants, shirts, socks and even a few boxers. I had also found a couple of gallon jugs of lemonade, one full and one over half empty, in the refrigerator and gathered up the remaining sodas and put them in a book bag.

"I found some clothes next door too," Elle said as we packed the duffel. "There's even a pair of jeans that might fit you."

"That would be great!" I had been feeling pretty out of sorts since I had dressed in the leisure suit style pants. I looked more like I belonged on a golf course with a bunch of retirees than on a survival quest in the wilderness. "Is your rifle a .22?"

"It is, but it's the only gun we have," she said with a very disappointed tone.

"What about that pistol that you had?" Thew last time I remembered seeing it, she had tucked it under the mattress.

"Don't be mad, but that was Bobby's, and it only had two bullets. I put it in with him before we buried him." She anticipated my anger at her actions, but in the time I had been with her, she had not even fired her rifle once though I knew that two guns would be better than one if we were ever overrun by a hoard of Takers.

"That's fine. I was just hoping you could use the shells I found." I placed my hand on her shoulder to reassure her.

I slipped the pack over my shoulder and snatched up the duffel bag and juggled with the two gallons of lemonade. Elle grabbed up the bag of sodas, opened the door and held it for me. I fumbled my way across the short distance and up onto the covered porch of the neighboring cabin. Elle opened the other door for me and I rushed in and quickly began to set everything down.

"Well, this stuff isn't too heavy, but it's too damn awkward." I stood in awe of the numerous packed bags on the living room floor of this cabin. "We're going to need a truck if we're going to take all of this stuff."

"I know." Elle shrugged her shoulders. "I wasn't sure how much you'd find next door, so I packed up as much as I thought we could both carry... and it looks like you packed more than you could carry too."

We spent the rest of the afternoon picking through our treasures and prioritizing until we were down to two backpacks, one duffel bag of clothes and other necessities, and one large travel bag that would be packed with the containers of water and drinks. We started up the generator and turned the power on to the air conditioner and the water pump. The relatively small cabin began to cool down quickly and was a comfortable temperature in the low 70's while we filled as many containers with water as we could fit into the designated bag.

"So, do you want to run a bath before we shut off the generator?" Elle asked with a smile. "It might be the last chance you have for a 'real' bath for who knows how long."

"Now that sounds like a brilliant idea!" I jumped into action and started running the water. "Where are those jeans you found?"

Elle guided me into the main bedroom. Displayed on the bed was a complete outfit, including boxers, socks, a long sleeved t-shirt and a glorious pair of jeans that were the right length and just one size to big around the waist. I couldn't help but smile at her thoughtfulness and I was truly in amazement of her ability to pack everything up and get clothes laid out. She had seemingly thought of everything, and I honestly knew I was more dependent on her than she was on me. She followed me down the hall and opened a closet door while I went to turn the water off. The tub was more than full enough and the water hadn't heated up much, but I knew it would be warm enough and very refreshing. Elle popped into the bathroom carrying a couple of towels and wash cloths. She hung one towel and one washcloth on the towel rack and handed the others to me.

"The sun's going to be setting soon. Don't fall asleep in here." She winked as she left the room and pulled the door nearly closed.

I soaked in the tub for a few minutes before I started scrubbing the grime away. It had only been a day since I had my last bath, but I felt like I really needed this one. While I was lathering up I heard the hum of the generator die and go quietly along with the air conditioner. I sighed thinking that I hoped I could sleep in the heat. When I finished washing up, I laid back and relaxed soaking in the cooling waters. I could hear Elle bustling around the cabin and figured she must be lowering the blinds and drawing the curtains to hide us from the Takers, should any wander through again tonight. I listened as she shuffled about and could hear her steps as she drew closer to the bathroom door.

"You almost done?" Her voice drifted softly through the slightly ajar door.

"Uh huh..." I said and began making splashing noises as I rushed myself out of the bathtub. "I'll be out in just a second."

Drops of bathwater pummeled the floor as I stood there drenched from head to toe. I snatched up the towel and dried off quickly. I soon realized that I had left all of the clothes lying on the bed. With my only other option being redressing in the dirty clothes, I chose to wrap the small towel around my waist and open the door the rest of the way. Elle stood in the hallway, leaning her shoulder and head against the wall.

"It's all yours" I smiled and felt my face grow flushed as I scurried past her to the bedroom where my clothes had been laid out so neatly. The sunlight was disappearing swiftly and the dim and dusky evening turned to night in mere minutes. I picked up the boxers and put them on, tossing the towel over the doorknob. I took the shirt, jeans, socks and shoes and carefully sat them in a nearby chair. Peeking out of the door and into the hall, I could see quite well in the pitch black and noticed the flickering light of a candle through the crack in the bathroom door. I flopped onto the thin mattress of the full sized bed, but it may as well have been a pillow-topped, king sized bed in a 5-star hotel. It was the most comfortable I could ever remember being. I'm not sure if I dozed off or if my mind had only wandered so far away that I lost track of time and of where I was, but I was drawn back to reality when I heard the deep gurgling sound of the draining tub.

Elle dried off as well as she could and wrapped herself in a baby blue, terrycloth bathrobe. Cupping her hand behind the flame, she blew out the candle and carried it into the front room. She ran her fingers through the tangles of her hair as she started down the hallway to the second bedroom, but stopped short and began to pace back and forth, biting her lip. Her brain told her she needed uninterrupted sleep with no distractions, but then that wasn't the only thing trying to persuade her. Elle had always been a bit of a tomboy and had become an unmovable rock of independence in the past few weeks, but under that callous façade was a soft heart that longed to just cuddle up with a strong man, and feel comforted and protected in his strong arms. There were other places that spoke to her also, tempting her in ways she hadn't even fantasized about until that very moment. The blood rushed to her face and all over sending uncomfortable tingling sensation to places that she could not ignore.

She stood in the doorway to my room and leaned against the door jamb reasoning with herself. *'I'll just lay down next to him...that's all.'* Elle chewed on her bottom lip and slid her hands up and around the back of her neck in contemplation. *'He's probably sleeping anyway... and if he wakes up, what's the worst that could happen?'* A devilish grin came over her chapped and pouty lips as she stepped into the room.

It must have been pitch black in the room because I watched her standing in deep thought and then walk into the room. My eyes were wide open and focused on her as she slipped off her bathrobe revealing every inch of her tan and toned body for me to see. Surely she didn't know that I was watching her so intently. I had to concentrate hard not to let out an audible moan at the sight of her beauty, sauntering slowly across the hardwood floor towards me. Every step revealed even more delectable details. Every line, every curve became more defined with every inch that decreased between us, until I could literally see the goosebumps of her naked flesh.

I lay as still as I could, not pretending to sleep, but trying to not be so obvious, in case, she could see me better when she grew very close. I half closed my eyes and peered through the slits of my eyelids and remained quiet until Elle crawled into bed next to me and curled her body vulnerably against mine, laying her head and hand on my chest. I could hold back no longer and I let out a groan of undeniable desire.

"You aren't fooling anyone, ya know?" Elle giggled quietly. "You've been watching me this whole time. Don't try to deny it."

"Huh?" I pretended to have no idea what she meant.

"Your eyes..." She paused for a moment and a wave of embarrassment came over me. "I could see them glowing from across the room... unless you're gonna tell me you sleep with your eyes open now."

"Ummmm..." I thought for a moment, but honestly, I had nothing. "Busted. Sorry, I just couldn't..." I was cut off mid-sentence.

"Shhhhh...." She quietly shushed me and placed her finger on my lips, soon followed by her lips.

Our arms soon snaked around each other moving about with wildly searching hands. I could feel her dulled fingernails and fingertips pressing hard into my neck and shoulders. Uncontrollably passionate kisses swept us away to a simpler time and place, a place that no longer existed anywhere but in our minds. My hands massaged and groped every inch of her neck and shoulders, working themselves toward the sensual small of her back as if they had a mind of their own. I rubbed and pulled my hands across the curves just below her waistline and then slipping carelessly down each side of her hips to her upper thighs. My hands cupped her buttocks tightly in their grip, kneading and massaging them while I began to kiss her ear and neck. Each moment filled the air with moans of delight as my kisses explored every inch of her flesh. Sudden moments of erotic magic caused her to tense and arch her back when my lips and hot breath invaded new erogenous places she had yet to discover, until a moment of unharnessed electricity shot through her. Her fingers drug through the tangles of my hair, grabbing and pulling when her body shuddered uncontrollably and then went limp.

"Stop..." She panted in a whisper. "I want you." She squeaked out quietly between gasps, coaxing me back, face to face. "I want all of you... now."

A billion thoughts and feelings flooded through my head, but only one word escaped my lips. "Yes."

I had no idea of what I was doing, but it felt so natural, I did not hesitate for a single moment. I suppose it truly is like riding a bike, even if you can't remember ever riding one. Both physical and emotional pleasures that exist only in thoughts and feelings, not words, immersed us in a sensual heaven that seemed to last for an eternity. The mundane reality of ticking time had probably only passed in minutes, but the seemingly endless waves of pleasure culminated in an erotic sensory overload. Our bare, sweat covered bodies, heaved with heavy breaths and indistinguishable, animal-like sounds. When our muscles stopped trembling and began to relax, we melted into each other... a romantic puddle of pleasure and contentment.

In time, we separated from each other as much as two adults can on a full sized bed. My eyes closed and my hand reached out for Elle's. I knew sleep was only moments away, and I was right.

CHAPTER 8

CAUGHT IN THE STORM

I found myself hiking a trail through an unfamiliar forest with a pack on my back and a jug of water in my hand. The sunlight filtered down through the tree leaves and cast a mystical glow on the flora below. While I walked I could sense that I was alone and searching for someone or something, but I was confused that it did not seem that I was seeking Elle. '*Who or what else could it be?*' I wondered. The daylight began to fade and fail, but it was not sunset. Clouds of charcoal gray began to roll in and thundering in the distance grew ever closer, so close and ominous that it began to shake the ground beneath my feet. A sudden crack of earth rumbling thunder and a blinding flash of lightning struck at my feet.

I sat straight up in bed trying to catch my breath and a cold sweat covered my forehead. I glanced over to see that Elle was stirring beside me.

"Ms. Elle, I'm scared." A tiny voice from the hallway broke the silence and I began to wonder if I was still deep in a dream within a dream. Elle awakened with a start.

"Did you hear that?" She whispered in a panic grabbing a handful of the flat sheet and covering herself.

"It's me, Maddie, Ms. Elle." The small voice drew closer and I saw the tiny child in the doorway. "Who is that?" She asked in a puzzled voice.

I quickly hid my eyes and said, "It's just me, Tanner."

"Oh, okay." Her voice was comforting. I actually missed the sound of people, even strangers, talking. "You have funny eyes tonight Mr. Tanner." She giggled.

"Where did you come from?" Elle asked the million dollar question.

"The cellar next door," She answered. "I hid inside of a big cooler when those Taker people came and took mommy and everyone else, but I just stayed quiet like a mouse... just like mommy told me."

"It was you?" I mumbled. "How did you get out of the cellar? I put a heavy chair over the door."

"All the thunder was shaking all the stuff and I got scared, and I was thirsty, so I just pushed and pushed and pushed." She sounded so oblivious to all that was going on like she was just home from a day in first grade and telling us about the picture she colored. "And so, I just got out and when I went outside the ground thundered and I could hear you in here making noises and I came to the back door."

"The back door was unlocked?" Elle asked and I think it was a question mostly directed at me, but Maddie answered.

"Yep! It was open, so I just came in." Her little feet took off in a four step run and she jumped into bed on top of Elle.

"Uhhh!" Elle groaned out when the little girl landed squarely on her stomach.

I reached down and pulled the blanket up from the floor next to the bed. Covering myself, I stood up and grabbed the pile of clothes from the chair.

"I'll be right back," I said quietly as I exited the room and disappeared into the other bedroom. I got completely dressed before returning with pillow and blanket in hand. Elle had done the same but had remained in the room with little Maddie. When I walked in, Elle was sitting on the edge of the bed, lacing up her boots and Maddie was still fully dressed and snuggled up in the bed. I laid the blanket out on the floor and put the pillow up near the head of the bed. Elle stood up, walked right up to me and wrapped her arms around me. She pressed her mouth against mine and offered up one last kiss before bed.

Elle joined Maddie in the bed and I curled up on the floor next to them. So much for a great night's sleep in that 5-star hotel bed. I hadn't been on the floor long when I heard the thunder rumble in the distance. I wondered if reality had been influencing my dreams, part of me wondered if this was all a dream and I would awaken, still in my boxers, to Elle telling me we had to get going. That did not happen. What happened was the next thunderous sound was much louder and closer, and the floor beneath me shook slightly. I sat up at the same time that Elle jumped from the bed and almost stepped on me.

"That's a Titan!" She called out loud. "We gotta go, NOW!"

"Well, shit!" I let the 's' word slip in front of the little girl. "Come on Maddie. We have to get going right now!"

"Hurry up! Grab some of the bags, whatever you can carry fast and let's get the hell outta here!" Elle was suddenly the tough drill sergeant woman I had met in the desert a few days ago... a few days? It felt like a lifetime ago.

The three of us stormed into the living room in a chaotic fury and began throwing backpacks and bags over our shoulders. Even Maddie snatched up a book bag and put it over her head and shoulder like a good little soldier. We rushed out into the night and saw the brilliant light of a nearing Titan approaching from the east, so naturally we ran west. Without a word we all headed into the evergreens. Maddie fought with the weight of the bag and soon began to fall behind. No second thought was given as I turned to snatch her up and carry her in one arm like a sack of groceries. We both froze in our tracks for a brief second as the Titan peaked above the tree line. Its brilliant light scanned the area and towered so high that it was slightly obscured by low hanging clouds. In that moment, I realized the incredible magnitude of our situation.

Ear-splitting, metallic screeches filled the air as its front appendage toppled trees and shook the ground with such intensity when it hit that we lost our footing and fell to the ground. With no more hesitation, I jumped to my feet and fled the monstrous machine as fast as my feet would carry me. I scanned ahead of me and quickly located Elle. I followed in the path she was blazing but continued to search our surroundings for some refuge. Just as I caught up to her, another horrible popping and screeching sound pained our ears.

"Tanner!" Little Maddie's voice screamed out in a high pitch that overtook the background din.

I turned to see her looking and pointing behind us. Just then the front 'foot' of the Titan slammed hard into the earth just short of the cabins. The size of this 'foot' alone dwarfed the cabins. I felt as if we were merely bugs scurrying to evade the careless footsteps of a human. I turned back to see Elle tossing her pack to the ground to gain speed and agility. Something ahead in the distance caught my attention. An outcropping of stone at the bottom of a high cliff wall to our right looked as if it might shield us from being noticed by the heat-seeking sensors of the Titan.

"This way!" I shouted, pointing to the right. Elle followed my lead and after a long sprint, we ducked under the outcropping to find that this three-foot tall opening dropped down a bit and nearly gave us room to stand up. We watched as the 'foot' of the Titan raised and moved forward, dragging slightly before it lifted. It completely destroyed the cabins and trees, sending huge logs and pieces of wood and furniture flying like scattering toothpicks. We instinctively ducked and hid our faces from the flying debris. I did not speak of it, but my thoughts turned to the horrific possibility that if a Titan stepped too close to our hiding spot, we could be buried behind tons of trees, boulders and dirt and sand. I didn't know what my beliefs were, but I prayed. I prayed to whoever would listen. I prayed to spare the life of this innocent child and the life of such a selfless woman who put others' lives and needs above her own. If I was spared by association, well, I wouldn't complain about that at all.

The earth shook again and again as the multistory building sized appendages landed and raised in sequence. In only a few stuttered movements the gargantuan structure passed by and was nearly over a mile away.

"Look!" Whispered Maddie excitedly. "That one isn't dark blue like the others."

"Yes, sweetie. It's a very pale blue... almost white." Elle stroked the small child's messy hair.

"Maybe it's sick. Momma said I look pale when I'm sick." Maddie was deep in thought on the subject, well, deep for a seven-year-old.

"I don't think machines get sick like we do," I whispered, half thinking aloud. "They break down and wear out, but it's a little different than being sick."

"Is it?" Elle asked. "You know we really know very little about the Ahsusha or the Takers, and nothing about the Titans.

"Yep! Maybe it's a Pale Titan because it's sick." Maddie reasoned as any elementary aged child would when confronted with enormous, robotic gorilla spaceships that had glowing gray, gelatine aliens at their helm.

"Well, so much for getting a good night's sleep and heading out in the morning." I pessimistically stated the obvious.

"There may be some truth to that, but I don't think we should go anywhere just yet." Elle cocked her head towards Maddie. "No reason you can't get a little shut eye, girl."

"Okay..." Maddie was less than happy about the notion of having to go to sleep. "But, I'm not even tired, really," She said with her chin on her chest.

I sat down the duffel bags, took off the backpack and unhooked one of the pillows from the pack and handed it to the tiny child. It took a bit of digging, but I managed to find a blanket in the duffel bag. Handing the plaid quilt to Maddie I remembered that Elle had dropped her bags to lighten her load so she could be quicker and more agile.

"I'll be right back," I whispered in Elle's ear.

"Where the hell do you think you're going?" She asked with a frown.

"I'm just going to go grab the bags you dropped." I smiled and kissed her forehead. "I'll be right back. I promise."

"You'd better be!" Her voice was hushed but forceful.

Elle watched and listened intently as I disappeared into the blackness of the night. She sat staring into the darkness awaiting my return with Maddie leaning against her. Nervously, Elle stroked the little girl's hair and counted the minutes as they crept by. When quite some time had passed, and just about the time she was beginning to worry, Elle heard a rustling in the distance. 'Finally!' She thought to herself. Squinting her eyes, she peered into the dark forest and looked for my silhouette to come into view. The rustling noises grew louder and multiplied. Through the darkness, she caught the movement of several figures meandering through the forest. 'TAKERS!' She screamed out in her head.

She pushed her lips up against Maddie's ear and whispered. "Takers are coming. Don't make a sound." She pushed the girl down against the ground and flattened herself out as much as possible behind the small uprising of ground between them and the Takers. They lay as still and silent as they could, even taking care to breathe quietly.

When the rustling sound of the Takers walking through the forest had seemed to pass, Elle cautiously reached for her rifle. She waited a few minutes and peeked her head over the dirt mound. Pressing the stock of the gun to her shoulder and looking down the barrel, she scanned as much of the forest as she could see. She sat poised and ready to fire if that became her only option. The sound of a gunshot would surely attract any nearby unwanted guests, but she was ready and willing to do what she had to do to save the life of Maddie.

It had now been quite some time and she had all but lost hope that I would ever return, but once again she heard a rustling. This time, it was coming from the direction the Takers had wandered. She listened as the sounds grew ever closer and she drew in a deep breath and held it when a figure appeared with glowing eyes. 'Damn you Tanner... you promised you wouldn't leave me.' the thought ran through her mind, but she wasn't angry; she was emotionally destroyed. Elle took her aim, slid her finger to the trigger and prepared to take her shot and then run with Maddie as fast as their feet would carry them.

***

I scanned around but saw no movement. With the stealth of a ninja cat, I stepped out into the dark forest. Okay, maybe it wasn't so ninja-like, but I was cautious and unobtrusive as I lightly strode away from our hiding place. I wandered in the direction that I believed we had come from searching the ground for the bags that had been discarded. The further I ventured, the more frequent I would stop and make sure I knew which direction the overhang was. I had mentally marked the area just a hundred yards away from the hiding spot as being an area of splintered evergreens where the rear appendage of the pale Titan had landed. It made for a fairly easy landmark to find. Nearly another hundred yards back near the location of another pale Titan 'footprint' I located the two large travel bags that Elle had dropped. I was a bit brokenhearted when I realized that flying debris from trees and large rocks had hit the bags. Scattered contents littered the area which was disheartening, but a feeling of distress overcame me when I noticed the second bag that had been filled with our containers of water was nearly destroyed and only a few containers remained intact.

I began to gather up the remnants of the supplies and shove them back into the travel bag. One or two items at a time, I cleaned the mess up and salvaged everything I could. I even shoved things into the bag that were most likely destroyed beyond use, just in case. I was nearly finished and on my hands and knees when I felt that something was amiss. The sound of rustling footsteps seemed to come from more than one direction. I slowly raised my head to the horror of a mass of Takers approaching. The first of more than twenty mindless slaves was only a few feet away. I prepared to spring into action and do my damnedest to be victorious over this battalion of 'alien-zombies'. My head swam and my stomach turned when the first of the takers passed by without even looking in my direction. One by one they passed me by as if I didn't exist.

About two-thirds of them had passed when I began to hear a very labored breathing approaching. There in the midst of the Takers, one stood out from the rest. It seemed more erect than the others, walked with more purpose in its steps and its eyes... its eyes glowed a pale gray color. The sound of its breathing grew louder as it approached and was sickeningly uncomfortable to hear. I stood still and did not budge when it passed within a few feet of where I was. It's raspy inhaling sounds of "A-a-a-a-a-a" and the wet gurgling sound of "Soooosh" as it exhaled repeated with every stride. Suddenly, I understood. Though I hadn't audibly questioned it, I had always wondered where such an odd name like 'the Ahsusha' came from.

When all had passed, I picked up the bags, and slowly followed them, walking like a mindless zombie. They seemed to be following the path of the pale Titan and that would lead them dangerously close to the hideout where Elle and Maddie could be quickly surrounded and trapped with a sheer cliff behind them. My racing heart eased when the path of the Takers drifted away from the cliff side of the Titan's trail and veered more to the left. I noted when we passed the 'landmark footprint' and shot sideways glances as we passed the cliff where I was pretty sure the girls were. It was quite a distance and I could not see them. I was somewhat relieved and somewhat concerned... perhaps they were completely out of sight, or maybe this wasn't the only herd of Takers that surged through the area. When the Takers began to ascend the other side of the first hill we had come to, I slowed my pace and fell behind intentionally. Slowing to a crawl and then stopping completely, I leaned against a tree and waited until all of the takers crossed the apex of the hill and disappeared on the other side. Even then, I waited another fifteen or twenty minutes before turning back towards the not so well-hidden hideout. I walked slowly and quietly, keeping a lookout behind and all around for any stray Takers that may be afoot. It had been over an hour by the time I approached the girls' hideaway. Even from thirty feet away, I could not see the girls at all. My concern grew into fear quickly, but I was actually relieved when I saw the head, shoulders and rifle barrel of Elle peek over the top of the small berm at the front of the overhang.

I raised my hands and bags in the air, and whispered loudly, "It's me, Tanner" knowing she did not have the benefit of built-in night vision. I watched as she lowered the gun and heard an indistinguishable whisper. I quickened my pace and saw the two girls lying flat on the ground behind the small berm which hid them much better than I had expected.

"You're back!" Maddie whispered with a smile.

"Yes, I'm back." I gave her a wink as I slid the two bags against the cliff wall and sat down next to Elle. It almost appeared that her eyes were watering.

"Don't you ever freakin' do that again," she whispered angrily in my ear.

"It wasn't planned, I swear... I did what I had to to make sure you stayed safe." I reassured her.

"You promised you wouldn't ever leave me." Her voice cracked as she spoke. "Don't. leave. me. alone." She paused between words, stressing the importance of each one. "Don't." Her raised pointer finger shook angrily in my face.

I wrapped my hand around the opposite side of her head and pressed my lips against her ear. "I promise." Though I knew it was a promise I couldn't guarantee. I wondered if it was a promise either of us could keep.

"Why don't you and Maddie get some rest. I'll keep the first watch and wake you if I get too sleepy, or in a few hours so I can get a couple of hours sleep before dawn." I said as I rubbed her back with my right hand, drawing out a quiet moan of pleasure.

"Don't start with me... you know how I get," She whispered in a devilish voice.

With a quick kiss, she left my side and joined Maddie on the cave floor. It seemed that in only a few short minutes the two girls were fast asleep and I was left alone with my thoughts. I listened as the warm breeze rustled through the pines and wondered if life would ever return to normal, or what 'normal' even was. I had only one real flash of memory, and that was of some sort of children's sleep over. I pondered the memory and every detail. Was it a childhood sleepover with my friends, or in some other life did I have children of my own? I searched the depths of my brain trying to find an answer, but there were no new revelations. Aside from the wind through the trees, the night had become eerily quiet. There were no sounds of nocturnal animals; no raccoons scurrying about, no night birds or owls fluttering by or calling out. The three of us seemed more isolated and alone than I could have imagined.

I began to wonder what the breaking dawn would bring. Where would our path lead us? Our water supply was diminished and as far as food... if we rationed very conservatively, we could probably survive for a week or so, at best. Desperation and depression began to overtake my thoughts. For a brief moment, I thought about walking away; leaving the two girls behind with all of the supplies giving them more food and water and possibly a better chance of survival, but I had made a promise, and right at that moment, I was relieved that I had. That was one choice I wouldn't have to make. I wasn't going to break my promise, and I certainly wasn't going to abandon them while they slept, even if it might give them both a better chance.

CHAPTER 9

THE DECISION

I sat still most of the night, alone with the voices in my head. In the pre-twilight hours, a nearby sound caught my attention. Elle was beginning to stir. It was a slow return to the conscious world for her. Hushed groans and awkward stretches brought the sleeping beauty back to life. I smiled as I watched her though I knew she must be pained after sleeping on the hard ground for several hours straight without even the slightest of movements.

"Good morning sunshine," I spoke softly. "Stiff this morning?"

"Morning?" Her eyes darted around, still filled with the sandman's sleep. "Is it almost morning? Why didn't you wake me up?"

"I wasn't really tired," I told a bold faced lie. "And you were sound asleep, so I just let you rest until you woke up on your own... or until the sun came up."

"It's starting to get light out already." She noticed, rubbing her eyes. "We had better get ready to get on the move."

"Yeah... about that." I wasn't sure how she would react or what she would say, but I had a thought. "What direction are we going? We never really had a chance to talk about it."

"I had an area map in one of the bags I packed. We need to take a look at it, see where we are, and head towards the closest town, I think." She caught me off guard.

"Oh. I didn't know you had a map. I was going to suggest we follow the trail of the Titan. There might be people in that direction that need our help... at least, that's what I was thinking." I waited for her rebuttal.

"We'll see if there's a town in that direction, but we really need to find someplace safe and a water supply before we go running off on some heroic quest to save the world." And this came from the most heroic person I had probably ever met.

"Holy hell, this is a mess." Elle began to search through the bag that I had recovered, but eventually, she produced a map, torn and wrinkled, but a map none the less. She handed me the wadded mess and went over to wake Maddie. "Time to wake up sweetie." She shook the little girl's shoulder, to which she received a tiny growl. "Do you want a cereal bar?"

The girl rolled over and managed to smile, nodding her head. While I opened and straightened out the map, Elle retrieved three whole grain cereal bars and one of the smaller containers of water. We all munched the bars as if we were having thanksgiving dinner, savoring every bite and being extra careful to not drop a single crumb. The twist-off lid was removed from a plastic soda bottle, which now contained a precious supply of water. We passed around like the treasured commodity that it was and took turns sipping from it. I actually packed toothbrushes and toothpaste, but I knew we couldn't spare any water for that right now. When we had finished, I capped off the water bottle and Elle rolled up the blanket and slipped the pillow back onto the backpack.

"Now... let's have a look at that map." She directed, noticing that it was growing light enough to see for her.

"Alright. Here it is. I looked at it for a minute, but I have no idea where we are." I was utterly lost.

"Hmmm..." Elle placed her index finger to her lip and studied the map for a few minutes. "Here." She ran her finger across a short distance. "This is the road down there, and here is where we were hiding in the cave before we came to the cabin, so we must be about here." She placed her finger on a specific point on the map.

"And there's Barnhill, right there." I drew her attention to a spot that marked a town on the map that didn't appear too far.

"True, but there is a cluster of short roads here. That's probably houses, like a subdivision." She made reference to another point about the same distance in the opposite direction.

"I don't want to argue, but I have to believe we have a better chance headed to a town, than what *might* be a group of houses." I raised one corner of my mouth and waited to hear her response.

"Okay..." She spun the map a quarter of a turn. "The direction we are looking is the way the map is laid out now." She rubbed her forehead. "So, the 'subdivision' is that way." She pointed in the direction that the Titan and the Takers had come from. "And Barnhill is in that direction." She pointed the opposite way, indicating the direction that the Titan had gone.

"Well... how far is it to either of them?" I asked.

"Um..." She looked at the legend on the map and used the width of her fingertip as a guide. "Looks like it's about 20-25 miles either way. With the three of us, it'd probably take four days to hike it, maybe longer depending on the terrain." Elle cocked her head to the side, noting that we would be traveling with a seven-year-old and that would most certainly slow us down considerably.

"I still think we should head to the town, but if you're dead set against it, then either we can ask Maddie, or toss a coin." I half smiled and raised an eyebrow. Elle drew in a deep breath and exhaled loudly.

"Logically speaking, there is nothing around that cluster of roads, and we are only assuming it's a subdivision or something. For all we know, it could be a campground. On the other hand, Barnhill is right on the edge of the map and we don't know what is beyond it..." She hid her face in her hands and slowly pulled them back, slightly stretching her cheeks. "So we load up and head for Barnhill."

"It makes sense when you put it that way." I smiled slyly. "You talked me into it."

Elle shoved my shoulder and slung two travel bags over her shoulders. With the overstuffed backpack in place, I grabbed up the duffel bag and stepped out into the morning light. Little Maddie slipped the book bag, filled with sodas, toiletries and first aid sundries, over her shoulder mimicking Elle and joined us. I knew the exact direction the Takers had gone and with the map and no compass I could only hope we would find Barnhill intact and not in splintered ruins and overrun with Takers, or the limp noodle remains of its residents.

We hiked to the top of the hill where I had left the Takers the night before. The view was not what I had hoped. A clear view for at least a few miles would have made our direction and path simpler to choose, but we found that the top of the hill was an illusion and after a short distance, the terrain began to climb even higher. Not only was our path slowed by the constant uphill climb, but with each mile we put behind us, the forest became denser. For lunch, we shared a can of ravioli and just before sundown we began to search for a hiding place. The forest was thicker now and our view was limited, but we were unable to find any real refuge. We found a place where the underbrush was heavy and made an open spot in the center of it all and took the time to have a handful of crackers and a can of vegetable soup for our dinner. I won't lie, by the end of the first day, I was famished and felt extremely undernourished.

The night was uneventful, at least, that was the report from Elle, who stayed up for more than half of the night so I could finally get some rest. During the first day, we followed the map towards Barnhill and the devastation of the Titan's path stayed to our left. Our path and its began to separate, which gave me some hope that we would find Barnhill intact. In the next few days that followed, the path of the Titan was gone from our sight and we did not have a single encounter with a Taker. The three of us began to talk more openly and in normal tones. It almost began to feel as if perhaps the worst was behind us and maybe soon we would find civilization and the world would return to normal. My strength waned as the days passed, but I persevered and pushed onward without complaining. With the passing of each hour and each day I grew more fond of my companions, we felt like some sort of misfit family; a half alien, a rebel beauty, and an orphaned survivor.

When the fourth day was coming to a close, and the sun was sagging low on the western horizon, we crested the peak of what felt like a mountain... what turned out to be more of a plateau. It was a true plateaued peak. The last fifty feet were a fairly difficult, overly vertical and no new tree growth. Once on top, I felt exposed and vulnerable. The plateau was covered in knee-high grasses, but aside from that, it was nothing more than an enormous open field. From this height, we could see in most directions for a fair distance. There appeared to be no sign of the Titan though I could see the trail of destruction it left behind, that wandered southwest for several miles before turning back north.

"Look!" Elle cried out; her arm jutted out to the distant western horizon.

"What is it?" Maddie's little voice questioned her but sounded more frightened than curious.

Immediately I knew what had elevated her morale and made her burst out loudly. I could clearly see geometric structures amidst the next clustering of trees. Barnhill was in our reach and did not show signs of being trampled by the Titan. There was a glimmer of hope in my eye when I looked at Elle and smiled. There was something different in her eyes... tears.

"It's Barnhill, honey," she said so sweetly to the child between us. "It's the town we've been looking for."

"Yaaaay!" Her tiny voice called out and she jumped as high as she could trying to see the promised land. "I can't see it." her tone dampened.

"It's still a long way off." I pointed out. "We won't make it before dark, and I'm not sure we should go there when it's dark. It just seems like it might be dangerous."

"Maybe." Elle said, but the way she said it made me think she disagreed.

"So, do you want to risk traveling at night?" I asked. "Do you think it would be safer to just stroll into town at night where we could be ambushed by those things?"

"You make a point," she admitted. "We could see them coming for a long way from here, but... we are also a wide open target. If they sense heat, or if the Titans do, we'd be sitting ducks out here."

"I wanna be a sitting duck!" Maddie said in a goofy voice and then giggled.

"No sweetie, you really don't." I grinned at her childish innocence. "Let's be walking ducks instead... let's walk that way." I pointed toward Barnhill and began to waddle in its direction.

"You two are insane." Elle threw her arms down to her sides and rolled her eyes, but she almost skipped as she caught up with us.

She was a tortured soul who knew what her heart told her was right, but also questioned her choices and worried about all of the 'what ifs'. Somewhere deep inside of her callous exterior was a tender young woman who still wanted to be a girl with nothing to worry about except perhaps: 'What would she wear on her date on a Saturday night?' Instead, she was the stitching that held the three of us together.

The blinding sun had turned a deep reddish-orange as it slipped to the edge of the horizon and then slowly sank behind it. We were closing in on the small town of Barnhill and my hopes sank as I realized that no one had spotted us and there were no sounds of cars zipping up and down the streets and into bicycle filled driveways, next to well-manicured lawns. The town was silent and as the daylight melted away, it was dark and dismal. There were no streetlights, no porch lights, no car lights, no lights in the ...

"Look!" I called out loud to Elle and pointed to one of the two story homes on the edge of the small burg that was only a few hundred yards away.

"What? Wha-d-ya see?" She was puzzled and looked back and forth between where I stood, stopped dead in my tracks, and the town.

"A light..." The adrenaline, or something, pumped through my veins and my heart pounded. "There was a light. I swear."

"Are you sure?" She wanted to believe me but hesitated in her optimism. "Where?"

"Right over there." I pointed again. "That two story house, right there. There was a light in one of the second-story windows, just when the sun went down."

"Are you positive?" Elle questioned my sighting again. "Could it have been just the sunset playing tricks?"

"I don't know... I'm pretty sure, but it disappeared so quickly." I began to second-guess myself.

With each step closer the silence and darkness grew heavier and hopes of finding anyone dwindled. I did maintain the hopes that we would find a safe place to 'hold up' and some food and other supplies. In our rush to flee the Titan, we had left behind some of the food and all of the spare clothing we had packed. I'm sure that after hiking for the better part of a week, I was not the only one who longed for a bath, even a cold one and a change of clothes... at least socks and underwear, and a fresh t-shirt. We chattered amongst ourselves about the probability of being the only people in this little village and about what we were most looking forward to.

"A bath... I am dying to take a bath." Elle's voice was perky and suddenly optimistic. "And a glass of wine."

"Me too." I agreed. "And some fresh clothes."

"Yes." Elle almost groaned the word out and then winked at me. "And then maybe another glass of wine."

"I want a peanut butter sandwich." Maddie grinned. Her wish was simple, but now, even the simple things sounded wonderful.

Elle stopped abruptly and put her hand out against the child's chest stopping her as well. I was one step ahead and turned back to see what had spooked her.

"Something wrong?" I whispered in a secretive tone.

"Yeah... Something moved up there." She didn't point or move. "It was low and it's so dark I can't be sure, but I swear something moved."

"If it's a Taker, they won't be hiding, right?" I tried to reason. We were so close I could almost taste that glass of wine and smell the peanut butter being spread on deliciously stale, old bread. "It's right there. Let's just be cautious, but we can't just stop or turn back now." I pleaded quietly.

"It just feels wrong, I don't know what it is, but something is watching us." Elle had never been this timid before, and I had no choice but to take her seriously.

"So, what do we do?" I asked for her advice on this troubling situation. "I mean, it can't be fifty yards away, so where do we go, what do we do?"

I looked back to the row of houses to judge the distance as I spoke and my eyes were fixed on a space between two of the homes. For a brief millisecond I thought I had seen movement too, and with my ability to see fairly well in the dark, I did not question it as much as I had Elle's sighting. A surprisingly loud "CRACK" split the silence and stung the left side of my chest, spinning me to the side. A wave of intense pain overtook me and my vision blurred as I crumpled to my knees. I could hear my heart pounding in my ears and it muffled the words of Elle and the scream of little Maddie.

"Dear god no!" She whispered out loud and dropped to her knees at my side. Elle had grown all too fond of having me around and was making mental plans of how our first night back inside of an actual house might play out, but those daydreams and plans were suddenly shattered.

Maddie remained standing with her face in her hands; a lone silhouette against the starry sky. "CRACK" without another sound, little Maddie wilted into the crisp grasses behind Elle.

"NOOOOOOOO!!!" Elle screamed out at the top of her lungs. "YOU BASTARD! SHE'S JUST A LITTLE GIRL!"

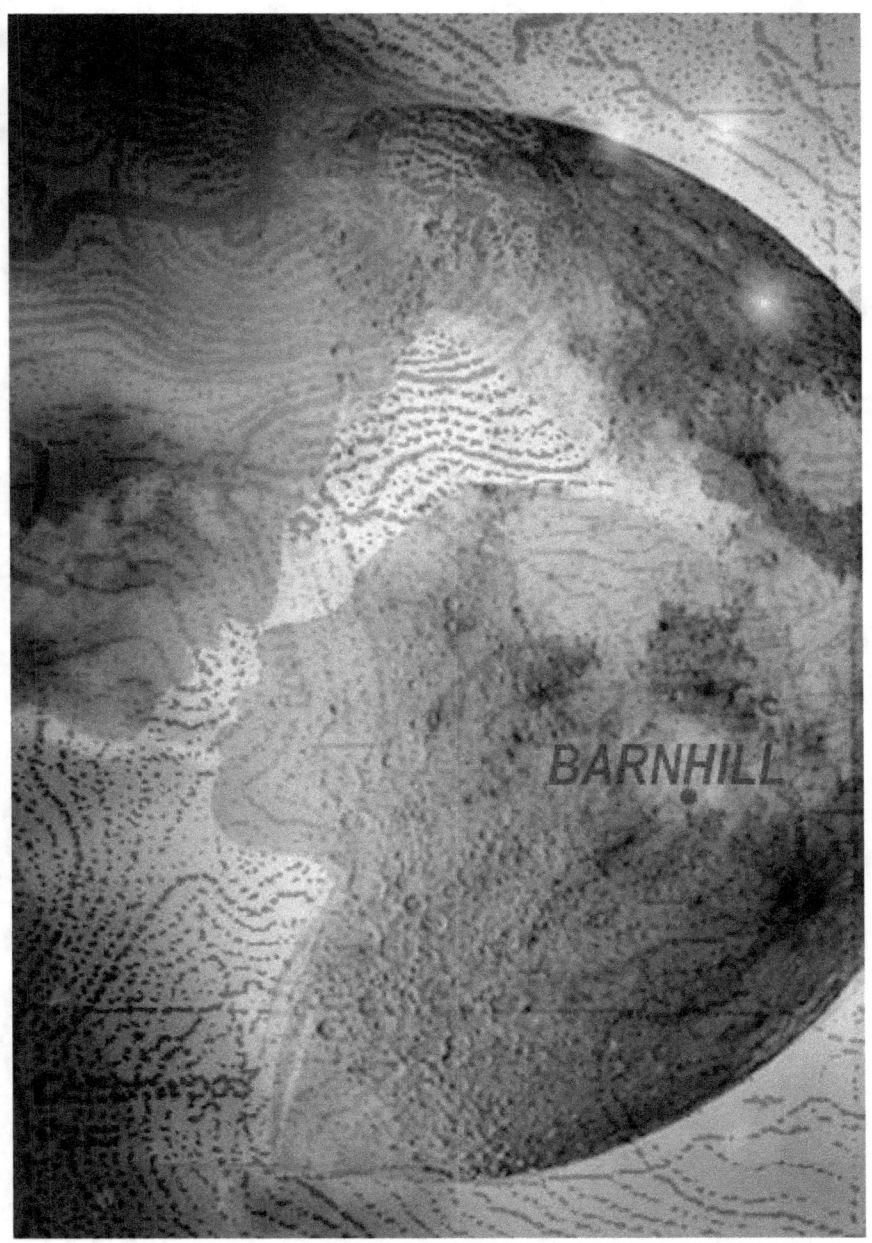

CHAPTER 10

PARADISE FOUND

The dark and silent night had been shattered by not one, but two devastating gun shots that shook Elle's world to its very core. I, on the other hand, had a burning and shooting pain in my chest that reduced me to an inanimate lump of flesh. The searing pain had blurred my vision and it seemed that I could not even breathe. Darkness overtook me, and for someone who had quickly become used to being able to see to some degree in the slightest of light, it was a bit terrifying. My muscles relaxed all at once and a voice from deep within told me to 'just let it happen'. It was a peaceful thought and the most frightening thing all at the same time. I knew it was my mind's way of telling my body that it was okay to die.

***

A young man came running toward Elle with pistol in hand. He stopped just short of her as she scooped up little Maddie in her arms and turned to face him.

"You're people?" The gun shook in his hand and his voice quivered as he spoke. "I mean, you are a normal person?"

"Yeah, unlike you... you murderer!" She yelled at him in such a condescending way that he dropped the pistol to his side. "Now, shut the Hell up and get out of my way!" Elle pushed past him and made a bee-line for the closest house.

"Where are you going?" She heard him say from behind her as she sped away. "And what about this thing? It's still alive!"

"What?" Elle froze for a moment before rushing forward again. "That's Tanner... he's a person just like me, and... he's alive?"

"A person?" The young man sounded confused. "But I shot because I could see his eyes glowing. How could he be a person and not one of those alien people?" He raised his gun again, putting Elle in its sights. "Just stop before I shoot you too. Something isn't adding up, and I don't trust anyone anymore."

"Then shoot me," she yelled at him over her shoulder. "I'm not stopping."

"Hey!" He shouted and took off running to catch up. "Wait up."

"No!" was all Elle said and she did not vary her course. The young man rushed past her and looked down at the child in her arms. Fear and horror struck his heart and he pointed to their left.

"In there. The front door is unlocked and we've got lights and stuff in the basement." He took the lead. "Follow me."

Elle was in shock when she processed the words that were spoken. Her world had crumbled around her in the past minute and hope suddenly sprung again with the single word 'we'. She followed the man into the empty home and realized she was putting her faith and trust into someone who had just shot the man she was falling in love with and a child. What was she thinking?

"You said 'we'. What did you mean?" Elle asked as they fumbled through the dark house to find the stairs to the basement.

"There are only six of us who didn't get taken when the alien-people-things flooded through here. There must have been a hundred of them." He opened the basement door and called out. "It's me, Jimmy. Need a light, NOW!"A striking sound was followed by a dim yellow light that grew whiter and brighter as he and Elle navigated the open wooden steps.

"Did I hear shots?" A woman's voice said from below.

"A child's been shot." Jimmy's voice was shaky and frightened.

"A child?!?" The woman in her mid-40's appeared at the edge of the stairs and took Maddie from Elle's arms. Elle began to shake all over, noticing her hands arms and shirt were covered in the crimson life of the child. Maddie's body was laid on a sofa-bed and was quickly surrounded by Jimmy and the two women. Elle fought her way next to the girl and took her cold hand in her own. A somewhat younger woman with dirty blonde hair and dressed in short sleeved yellow pullover and a pair of jean shorts took off with a shot through a door into a separate area of the finished basement. In mere seconds, she reappeared with her arms overflowing with an array of first aid supplies.

"She isn't breathing!" The woman who took her from Elle said with the urgency of an emergency room nurse. "Back up!" She motioned with her arms and then began to perform CPR.

The dirty blonde ignored her order and after dropping armloads of supplies, ripped open two packages of gauze and pressed it firmly against the bullet wound in the child's abdomen. The room began to spin for Elle, her head was dizzying and she began to feel nauseous. She toppled against Jimmy and as he caught her she mumbled. "Tanner... Tanner's shot too." as if she were reminding herself just before she passed out.

Jimmy helped the lifeless Elle to the floor and placed a small pillow behind her head. "Angie, c'mon. I need help... hurry."

***

"Where're we going?" Angie asked as she trotted up the stairs trying to keep up with Jimmy.

"There's a guy out here... he's been shot too," Jimmy admitted. "I'm not sure he's... 'normal' though."

"What's that supposed to mean?" She asked curiously as they burst out the front door.

"I was out here keeping watch when I saw them coming across the open field." He began to recant the story. "When they got close enough, I could see that glow in his eyes, so I shot. The woman inside fell down with him, but not the girl, so I shot again. I thought they were coming back for us."

"What makes you think this is okay? Why should we help that thing?" Angie slowed down as they approached the body that lay still in the grass.

"The woman who carried the child inside... she said he was a normal person, just like her." Jimmy fought with the reasoning, but his gut told him to trust Elle, a stranger who had collapsed in his arms.

"Then I think we should take him to the other safe house." Angie thought keeping him isolated might be the safest thing for their small clan. "If he's still alive, that is."

Jimmy drew his pistol as they approached the man who laid face down on the grass. Angie squatted down over the body and gently laid her fingers on the side of his neck, just below his jawline. She held them there for several seconds and cocked her head to the side almost as if she were listening for something.

"There's a pulse," she said softly, fearing they may not be alone. "I'll take his feet if you can get his head." She rolled the body of the man onto his back.

Jimmy slipped the pistol back into his shoulder holster, slid his arms under the armpits of the injured man and wrapped them around his chest. Angie put one leg on either side of her hips and took hold of his ankles. The two clumsily carried the man nearly a block away, with several stops along the way to rest and recover their grips. When they made it to the second safe house, Jimmy and Angie laid the man on the porch while he dug into his front pocket for the key. When the door was unlocked and swung open, they picked the man back up and carried him inside. The injured and limp body was laid out on the kitchen floor. Angie searched blindly through the cabinet drawers, looking for a clean dish towel while Jimmy went up to the second story and opened the blind on the south wall of the master bedroom. Slipping a disposable lighter from his pocket, he flicked the flint-wheel under his thumb and lit the flame for a count of two seconds. He paused and repeated the action three times when he saw a flash of light from the distant treeline.

***

Elle was confused and disoriented when she felt a hand gently shaking her shoulder. The inescapable darkness blinded her and moments of dream and reality, rationality and illogical fantasy flickered through her mind like movement in a strobe light: Bits and pieces of her life, her family and friends before the alienation, glimpses of memories made with Tanner, illusions of a life with him that had never existed outside of her hopes, the woman and the children in the cave... Maddie! Like the crack of a whip she was awake and present.

"Tanner, is that you?" She wondered if I was okay, but soon realized she did not see my eyes glowing in the murky blackness. "Who's there?" Her hands and feet shuffled backward, on her butt sliding against the cold concrete floor.

"It's me... Jimmy" A familiar voice, that she could not place, said. "We met outside when I shot..."

"Where are they?" Elle spat out in anger. "Where are my friends?"

"The girl is in the next room." His voice sounded desperately somber. "Sh-sh-she's..."

"No, she isn't!" Elle shouted in the darkness, cutting him off, mid stutter.

"Well, n-no, but she's not doing too good... not good at all." His voice was quiet and remorseful. "I'm sorry. I thought I knew, but I didn't know... Hell, I don't know anything anymore. I was s-s-s-so scared."

"And Tanner?" Elle almost felt sorry for the young man.

"They took him to the other house," he spoke as if she knew what 'the other house' meant. "I'll take you there if you want."

"I wanna see Maddie first." Elle's voice was calmer now, but still demanding.

"Of course," Jimmy said, "Right in here."

Elle heard the rattling sound of a doorknob and the squeaking hinge of a seldom used basement door. The striking sound of a disposable lighter gave a bright glow to a very small area of the doorway and Elle followed it like a spirit drawn to the warmth of the light on the other side. She followed it diligently into the next room where she saw the middle-aged woman, who had been performing CPR on little Maddie, sitting in an uncomfortable looking chair at the child's bedside. No movement could be seen, in the faint flame-light, from the child's form as it lay silently on the fold out sofa-bed. The lighter grew too hot for Jimmy to keep his thumb on it any longer and he let go, putting them in blinding darkness.

"Sorry," Jimmy whispered. "Gimme a minute." Elle heard him blowing on the lighter wheel to cool it down.

"It's okay," Elle said calmly. "I understand."

"They have the crank light at the other house." The woman in the chair said. "By the way, I'm Maryanne."

"Nice to meet you, Maryanne. I'm Elle." She felt odd speaking into the darkness and not being able to make eye contact.

"And I'm..." Jimmy began, but Elle cut him off again.

"Jimmy... yeah, I know." Elle was less than interested in Jimmy, or what he had to say. "Maryanne, I don't remember much, but I do remember seeing you helping Maddie. Thank you."

"Maddie," Maryanne said out loud. "What a lovely name for such a lovely young girl." She realized her error and said, "Is Elle a name or an initial?"

"Name." She smiled in the darkness. "Like the woman's magazine."

"I like it very much Elle," Maryanne spoke very softly. "It is a pleasure to meet you, even under such horrible circumstances... just nice to know we aren't all alone. You'll have to tell me all about you and your story... and how you found us." The woman rambled a bit before Elle broke into her monologue.

"Eventually, maybe... how is Maddie?" Elle cut right to her point. It's all she really wanted to know right at that moment.

"Hard to say," Maryanne spoke as Jimmy flicked the lighter on again and Elle took the opportunity to rush to Maddie's side. "She's breathing on her own, but her pulse is very weak. She may have lost a lot of blood and we did our best, but she's still bleeding some."

"You've got to make it sweetie... I need you." Elle took the child's hand in hers and felt the clammy chill in it. Turning her head toward the woman, she noticed the silver flecks in her hair. "Is she going to be alright?"

"I wish I could tell you, yes, but I'm no doctor, and this isn't even close to a hospital. We do have a small clinic on the other side of town... maybe a mile or so." The woman looked off into the empty dark corner of the room, deep in thought. "If she is still with us in the morning, we'll move her there and maybe we can do more for her then. It's too risky to move at night. There used to be more of us, you know? There were eighteen the first day after. Now, just six." She reached out and touched Elle on the back of the head, stroking her hair. "Don't be so hard on Jimmy. He was just trying to protect us... doing what he thought was right."

"Jimmy..." Elle mumbled the name. "Take me to Tanner now."

"Tanner?" Who's Tanner?" The woman questioned Jimmy.

"Later. It's a long story." Jimmy said as he let the lighter go out again.

"It's a longer story than you know... maybe I'll tell you sometime. Nice to meet you, Maryanne. I'll see you again soon." Elle seemed confident.

Jimmy blew on the lighter again and fumbled through the dark until he found the stairs. "When I light the lighter again, come here and head up the stairs as quick as you can."

He stood still for a minute while the lighter cooled down and then he whispered. "Ready?"

"Ready." Elle echoed as the tiny flame cast its shadowy glow on the lower steps.

She rushed to the top of the stairs and took two steps out into the hallway just as the light went out again. Rapid thuds signaled Jimmy's ascent of the steps in his sneakers. He whispered to Elle, "Follow me... grab my shirt if you need to." Elle almost resented the statement, but the angel on her shoulder told her he was only trying to be considerate. She followed closely behind him to the front door and then through it and out into the open night. The two crept from bush to house, to behind cars and even trash cans as if they were crossing a dangerous war zone... which is literally what they were doing.

Elle hadn't been able to keep track of how many houses they had passed, but they hadn't traveled more than a block, at least, they hadn't crossed a street. Elle followed Jimmy up onto a small concrete front porch and listened as he knocked three times lightly, paused, knocked once, paused again and then knocked three times lightly again. They stood tight against the front of the house, as quiet at church mice, and waited to hear an answer. No footsteps were heard, but soon the metallic click of a deadbolt unlocking drew their attention and they stared as the door swung open quickly and an elderly man poked his head out.

"Hurry." was all he said and disappeared back inside.

The two entered the home and the old man reached out to them in the dark. He clumsily groped in the dark and at length took them by the arms and led them to the back of the house where they stopped. Letting go of them, he opened a door that swung away from them and a cold and pale glow filtered up from the lower level of the home.

"Lot of bedrock around here." The old man said as he began to descend the stairs one at a time. He paused and looked over his shoulder. "Not many houses with a basement to hide in."

It seemed to take forever, but they finally reached the bottom of the stairs and Elle saw something she hadn't seen in what seemed like a lifetime- a flashlight. Her eyes scanned the dimly lit space from right to left and was filled with touches of micro-nostalgia. An old yellow-orange flower print couch lined the wall to the right, with a slender, elderly woman in a house dress and blue, plush slippers sitting on one end and a fat, white Persian cat sprawled out on the other. In front of the couch was a worn out, scratched and dulled rectangular maple coffee table. It looked like something that was once straight out of a 1970's Sears and Roebucks catalog. The flashlight rested on it and in its fading beam, dust sparkles danced and drifted down onto a scattered arrangement of cello wrapped hard candy... Butterscotch. Elle wanted to reach out and grab one up and just smell it. It had only been a few weeks since the world had gone to hell, but she already missed the simple things that had been taken for granted for so long, by so many. Her eyes were soon drawn away across the Berber carpeted floor to the far left side of the room where an air-mattress held her only real friend, who lay still, under a plain, flat sheet.

Elle, without a word or introduction, darted to the side of the air mattress, knelt down and laid her hand on the chest of her new found companion. Her mind denied, to her heart, that she was falling for this odd stranger, but there was an undeniable comfort when she felt the shallow murmur of a heartbeat in his chest. A tear rolled slowly from the corner of her eye as she leaned over and rested her head on his chest and listened contently to the faint sounds of life. Jimmy wanted to speak and explain who this silent stranger was, but he stood quietly and watched the emotional reunion along with the others. He looked at Elle in the dying light and could almost see the care and sorrow pouring out of her like the two were becoming one. The elderly man sat down on the couch, placing the fur-ball onto his lap and the silver-haired woman rested her head on his shoulder. Knowing of the little girl at the other safe house, she wondered if this had been a wandering family and if there might be other survivors.

CHAPTER 11

BLINDING PASSION

After a lengthy rest, Elle was jolted back to the present by a whirring sound. She opened her eyes and lifted her head to see the light growing brighter and bouncing off of the walls and ceiling. Rubbing her eyes, Elle ruffled her fingers through her jet black hair and saw the elderly gentleman cranking away at the emergency flashlight. When he had finished, he placed it back on the coffee table and Elle found that she had become the center of attention.

"I didn't mean to be rude, but right now Tanner and Maddie are all that matter to me," She spoke honestly. "I'm Elle."

"Tanner? Is that his name?" The silver-haired woman asked and Elle nodded. "I'm Jean, and this is my husband Ed. We've been married for thirty-seven years... and you already met Jimmy."

Elle simply bobbed her head up and down, taking it all in, and then silently lipped the name 'Jimmy' repeating after Jean, but getting her first good look at the tall and slender man. She sized him up to be about six foot two inches, or so and probably in his very early twenties. His hair was short, blonde and curly and he had the appearance of having attempted to be clean shaven, but he had a gruff two or three-day shadow.

"I... I... don't know how to tell you how sorry I am." Jimmy stuttered in a child-like way that Elle found genuinely sweet.

"I understand." Her voice was firm, and not forgiving, despite her words. "It was a mistake... but it was a stupid, chicken-shit mistake. You could have waited until we were closer and asked us to stop or something."

"He was only trying to protect us." The elderly gentleman, Ed, spoke with a voice as smooth and silky as a late night radio announcer. "It may have been a bad mistake, but it wasn't on purpose."

"You have every right to be angry, furious in fact," Jean said. "Jimmy could have killed your little family, and it's still iffy. He... Tanner is doing better than he should be, but he isn't outta the woods yet."

"Better than he should be?" Elle asked curiously.

"Yep," Ed answered back. "He not only stopped bleeding, but his would is already healing up. Can't explain it, but well... there it is."

Elle thought about the expedited healing of Tanner's leg after his brush with the Ashusha, but knew that a cut on the leg was completely different than a gunshot to the chest. She didn't mention anything to the new people about the unusual changes he had undergone since his encounter.

"Ed and I are going upstairs to get some sleep." Jean said and moaned as she stood up. "Make yourself at home. There's the couch here, or there's a spare bedroom upstairs if you want."

"I'm just going to sit here on the couch. I'll stay awake while you all get some rest." Jimmy offered, but Elle thought it was most likely out of guilt.

"I'm Just going to sit here too. I'm not leaving him until morning and then I'm only going to go check on Maddie." Elle announced firmly.

"It's safer down here anyway." Jimmy pointed out. "At least, have a seat here..." He patted the open couch cushion. "It's a lot more comfortable than the floor." Elle reluctantly joined him and the time slipped silently away. She struggled to stay awake, but the old couch that had the appearance of a second-hand store reject was far more comforting than she could have imagined. The blinking of Elle's eyes grew more frequent and with each blink, they remained closed slightly longer, until her strength and her ability to hold her eyes open faded in perfect synchronicity with the dimming of the crank-light.

TANNER:

The stinging pain in my chest shot through every cell of my body and the stars above me spun. My mouth watered and a familiar, sickening metallic taste filled it. My stomach turned when some distant memory took over my senses.

I was maybe ten years old and chasing a yellow-haired boy through a wooden privacy fenced yard, filled with thick green grass. The sun shone blindingly down on us as we played carelessly in the magic of summer. Grabbing the corner of the redwood stained picnic table, I sped faster than humanly possible making a hairpin turn, imagining I was a superhero with lightning speed. My childhood friend and arch-enemy/super-villain was nearly in my grasp when I became a victim of his secret weapon, a booby-trap so ingenious, I was completely unprepared for the crushing blow it dealt... the dreaded sprinkler trap! I slipped on the long, wet grass where the yard sprinkler had soaked it with its oscillating, arching streams. Before I could even blink, my feet flew to the side and off of the ground. I was briefly airborne before my hands and face met sharply with the ground. My eyes welled with tears and the world around me became a watery blur. The wind had been knocked out of me and as badly as I wanted to cry out, I had no breath. My ribs ached as I raised and lowered my chest, trying to fill my lungs with precious air. Wiping the tears from my reddened cheeks, I sniffed in deeply and that is when I felt a new pain that I hadn't noticed until that very moment. I had busted my nose and split my lip wide open. At ten years old, I was sure I was about to die a tragic, yet heroic death that would be written about in an epic comic book and the story told at sleepovers and cookouts for years to come. I rolled onto my back and glared up at the summer sky. Everything began to turn off-kilter and I wasn't sure if I would puke or pass out when I noticed something odd. The sun had been hiding behind a full sugar-maple tree, but now there were three suns, or that is what I was hallucinating. One sun even larger than normal, and two smaller ones on either side. I watched as they appeared to grow closer, brighter, larger... filling my sight with a light so brilliantly white that it washed away all color from my sight. My muscles tensed uncontrollably when I choked on the liquid that had begun to pool in my throat. My involuntary reaction had forcefully expelled a spray of blood out of my mouth, which to the other boy, who had come to see what happened, was probably either the coolest or the single most frightening thing, he had ever witnessed... and there it was, that putrid, rich metallic taste. Blood... my mouth was filling with blood.

The pain left with my consciousness and it only seemed like the blink of an eye when I was aroused by a very passionate kiss. I opened my eyes and my gut knotted up immediately. It must have shown very clearly in the expression on my face.

"What's wrong? Did you have a bad dream, or are you feeling sick again?" A beautiful woman with sandy brown hair said and pushed out her lower lip in a pout.

"Serena?" The name came to me the instant I heard her voice. I opened my eyes to find that I was sitting next to my wife on a large airliner. My wife? My head spun and I really did begin to feel sick to my stomach.

"I shouldn't have woke you up. I'm sorry." She said and took my hand in hers. "But look, isn't it beautiful?"

She leaned her head against the plane's window and gazed out and I could see the awe in the sparkle of her eyes. I leaned over her and peeked out. It was unlike anything I could have imagined and more brilliant than any photograph could have ever captured. Pinks, purples, oranges, and reds had painted the most amazing sunset over the desert below, and the view from this height was indescribably beautiful. Without warning, a sharp pain struck, like someone had jabbed an ice-pic down through my skull, frontal lobe, and its pressure throbbed behind my left eye, with such intensity that it felt as if my eye could burst out of its socket. In perfectly synchronized time, a brilliant flash of light appeared in the sky overhead. Instinct pushed me to squeeze my eyes closed with a pain-induced flinch, but there was a force greater than the pain that had my stare fixated on the unidentified luminous object. The light grew larger and suddenly two smaller lights appeared just behind it. The plane shook violently for a moment and the lights flickered.

"Ladies and gentlemen, this is your Captain speaking." A very masculine voice came over the intercom. "We seem to have hit some turbulence. Please fasten your seatbelts and put your trays in their upright positions."

"Babe..." Serena nudged me. "Did you hear the pilot?"

I heard, but I ignored his request. I was spellbound by the brilliant lights that were speeding through the sky and growing larger and brighter with every passing millisecond. Fear reached deep into my chest and squeezed my heart so angrily that I became paralyzed. The objects grew closer and larger until the closest one dwarfed the jet. The plane shook again in a constant and furious vibration and the interior lights failed and went dark. Our momentum seemed to be slowed and I knew, without knowing, that the planes jet-engines had all lost power. Even with this terrifying possibility, I could not take my eyes off of the geometric meteor that was overtaking us. The temperature of the cabin quickly rose and the light from the glowing object lit up every window. The entire jet vibrated convulsively and without warning everything went blindingly black and every sound was pulled from existence like we had entered the inescapable vacuum of a black hole.

Once again, I was startled to reality by a warm kiss and the gentle touch of a hand on my face. I opened my eyes, but all remained black. I reached out through the void and found her. My arms wrapped tight around her and I trembled in fear.

~*****~

JIMMY:

Jimmy sat quietly next to Elle, thinking how this woman and her two companions had stumbled carelessly into his little town in the middle of the night. Her presence had given him a sudden hope that there must be others, and his 'knee-jerk' reaction to seeing them approaching had emotionally scarred him like a searing cattle brand, charring 'GUILT' into his soul. Flashing memories began to fill his thoughts. It seemed that was all he had now... memories: Outbursts of anger over losing his job after the economy's recent recession, cussing and screaming when he found a new grocery cart dent in the door of first pickup truck, even though it wasn't the only dent; rarely hugging his aging grandmother and forgetting to call her on her birthday; falling in love with a petite ginger-haired girl with more freckles on her cheeks and shoulders than there were stars in the sky and having her ripped from his life without warning. So much of Jimmy's life had been spent misdirecting energies and misunderstanding emotions. Life had gone from a complex world where every waking minute mankind had bombarded itself with amazing technology filled with mostly pointless information, and each day held new options and decisions, and every simple action could open a floodgate of possible reactions, to a life that was now the simplest of existences and the only decisions that had to be made were ones that would provide a meal or preserve a life. Jimmy felt that his little town had come full circle to the dawn of man; living in darkened 'caves', staying hidden from the wild beasts that would kill them, and hoping they were lucky and skilled enough not to starve to death.

Unlike the voice of his past, that chattered away relentlessly in his head, there were no sounds to fill the empty room. While he sorted through his regrets, his eyes drifted to Elle and as her exhaustion pulled her slowly into a sleepy abyss, he watched the stress and tension slip away from her. She pulled her feet and legs up to her and tucked her arms in tight. Even though the basement room was a very comfortable temperature, Jimmy thought she looked chilled, curled up next to him in an almost fetal position. Reaching over her, he pulled the afghan down from the back of the couch and unfolded it, wrapping her gently in it. Elle squirmed momentarily, making unintelligible sounds of comfort, like a child cuddling with its favorite teddy bear. When Elle settled back into her sleep, she had wiggled her way over and was using Jimmy's thigh as a pillow. It was a moment of indecision, but the longer he thought the easier it was to choose. He sank into the couch took a deep breath and put his past out of his mind. Softly, he laid his arm across her and put his hand on hers, feeling the perfection of her supple skin, marred by scratches and callouses from the harsh reality of recent events.

The two strangers melted together as the dark night passed ever so slowly as if the sun were afraid to show itself to our cruel world. Jimmy slid lower and lower, slouching further over and Elle readjusted with every change. Elle rustled, half awake, and found herself wrapped in a pair of strong and caring arms. With no other thought, she squirmed against the firm body behind her, and in her sleepy mind, she saw Tanner. Her hand ran the length of his thigh and she turned awkwardly on the narrow couch. His hand touched hers and then massaged its way up her arm and shoulder, reaching the small place on the back of her neck that sent her heart racing. The hesitation lasted but a second before he kissed her... and she kissed him back, a hard, passionate, intentional kiss. His fingers ran through her hair and she pulled him against her hard. Loud and deep breathing filled with moans of pleasure began to fill the room when he began to kiss her neck and explored her curves clumsily.

A near silent hum came from the flashlight on the coffee table. Being the only other sound in the room, the two noticed but paid little attention to it. When the light hummed again, only louder, Elle snapped back from her paradise of passion.

~***~

ELLE:

"What the Hell are you doing?" She pushed Jimmy away and fell onto the floor. "What gives you the right to touch me like that?" Her fury was directed at Jimmy, but inside, she knew she was talking to herself for being so willing to be held and touched intimately.

"I thought you..." Jimmy didn't know what to say, and with his own insecurities taking over, he believed he was completely at fault.

"Well don't think again." Her words stabbed at him cruelly. "Keep your distance or, so help me God, you won't live to..." Just then, the flashlight made a buzzing sound on the table and vibrated onto the floor.

"What the Hell was that?" Jimmy asked. "Did you feel that?"

"That's a fucking Titan!" Elle said. "...and I think it's getting closer."

"A Titan?" Jimmy sounded confused. "What's a Titan?"

"One of those giant mechanical *'things'*. You know... the things those aliens landed in." Elle was frustrated at his ignorance.

"ALIENS!?! We were overrun by those zombie people. There were some of them that had a light in their eye that I could see and they seemed to be leading the others, and taking everybody... but giants? I didn't see any giants." Jimmy tried to make sense of it all in his head.

"Damn it, I'm still pissed at you, but I don't have time for that right now." Elle began. "Okay... there were these giant ships that landed or crashed, we call them Titans. The 'aliens' were like glowing jello things and when the take over a person the person has this weird breathing noise that sounds like 'aaaaa- sooosh-aaaa-sooosh'... so I started calling them Ahsusha. They are the people with the glowing eyes. The ones that they take over and then leave like zombies, they are like an army bent on taking or killing the rest of us. They are the Takers. The Titans are so huge that when they move the earth shakes like an earthquake. That is 'what the Hell' that was."

"Okay... so what do we do?" Jimmy asked nervously. "We've always just kinda hid out and tried to avoid the... Taker things."

"What we do, is hope like hell that they don't come here. If they get close enough for us to see them, they'll probably see us too, and then we can't get away fast enough." Elle's eyes glazed over when she thought about the invaders and how many people she had known or encountered that had not escaped them. Elle did not want to be part of those growing numbers and had a momentary urge to abandon everyone and run. It wasn't her nature, but she had seen with her own eyes, in a 'fight or flight' situation, few had won the fight.

There was a buzzing again, but Elle couldn't tell if it was stronger than the last. The only thing she was sure of was that there was a Titan on the move and it was close enough to rattle this little town. Elle snatched up the light and gave the handle a rigorous cranking until the light glowed brightly. She waved the light around to get her bearings. When she spotted the motionless form of Tanner on the under inflated air mattress, she sat the light on the table and moved to his side. She sat on the hard floor next to him and brushed his hair to one side with her fingers. He moaned lightly and turned his head toward her. It was the best sign she had been given since the shooting. A single laugh escaped her lips just as a tear of joy was freed from her eyes. Elle was drawn to him and she leaned in close and kissed him.

I slowly came to consciousness and I ached in every cell of my body, but there was the most comforting peace that came with a warm kiss that I did not expect.

"Serena. I'm so glad you're okay." I mumbled groggily.

"Serena?" The familiar voice said unhappily.

"Elle!" The name sounded like coming home. "Sorry... I was having the weirdest dream. I was on a plane with someone named Serena, and I think we were about to crash when you kissed me."

"And you thought that it was 'Serena' kissing you and you were glad she was alright?" Elle was obviously upset and jealous.

"I guess so... but it was just a dream... a nightmare really. I thought I was about to die. The plane was being hit by a meteor or something." I tried to remember, but the details were starting to slip away into a foggy forgetful place. "Where are we?"

"We made it to Barnhill," Elle said, knowing it was not the paradise we had hoped to find.

Just then a loud rumbling filled the basement and the earth shook violently. Jimmy rushed through the door and up the stairs, calling back over his shoulder. "I'm going to check on Ed and Jean."

"Who was that?" I asked, filled with confusion.

"I'll introduce you to everyone if we get the chance." There was fear in Elle's voice. "There is a Titan coming. We need to go."

"The pale one? ...I have to find it." I don't know where the words came from, but I knew that there was an urgency deep inside that I couldn't ignore. "There was a pale Titan and I need to find it."

"You aren't thinking straight." Elle tried to reason. "We don't want to find any of them. We have to get Maddie and get out of here."

"Where is Maddie?" I asked, still shaking off the confusion of my dream.

Before Elle could answer, Jimmy and the elderly couple came rushing as swiftly as they could into the basement. Again the earth quaked beneath our feet and all around us. The Titan was dangerously close now, too close to risk an escape on foot. Maddie and the others were blocks away at another 'safe house' and we had no way to contact them without physically leaving our safe haven and chancing the trip outside. I looked at Elle without a sound and with a quick nod, I darted for the stairs. She took off behind me, leaving the others behind, wondering if we had lost our minds. Reaching the main floor of the home, we could see the struggling light of the early morning sun creeping in through the heavy plaid curtains.

"Where are we going?" I asked Elle.

"I was following you," she replied curiously. "Where *are* we going?"

"To get Maddie," I answered her. "And then we have to get you two someplace safer."

"I think I can find the house, but I can't be sure." Elle peeked through the window curtain next to the front door.

I took Elle by the hand, unlocked the deadbolt and gave the brass knob a twist. I swung the door open and pulled her out into the perilous world. Elle pulled the door closed behind her and we trotted across the porch, down the steps, and into the unshielded front yard. Elle stopped suddenly, looking around at the strange and silent neighborhood. Low, misty gray clouds enveloped the town and gave it the feel of a post-apocalyptic movie set. It was an eerie feeling to see such a desolate world, cars were still parked in their places, bicycles lay in the front yards, and trash bins lined the street awaiting a garbage truck that would never come.

"None of this looks familiar." Elle's voice cracked and I felt her hand tense in mine.

"We can't just stand here. We either go back inside, or we try to find Maddie." I stated what seemed obvious to me just as a metallic creaking echo reverberated through the sky above us.

"RUN!" Elle screeched out and pointed to the sky above the line of cracker box houses that lined the street. Just above a thick layer of low-hanging clouds, through a wispy, foggy and more transparent layer, a metallic, midnight blue structure could be seen. One of the darker Titans was no more than a few miles away. I clenched Elle's hand in mine and followed her lead as she took off in a sprint to her left, darting between two beige, vinyl sided homes. We ran quickly through backyards filled with swing sets, swimming pools and a barrage of patio furniture. We ducked under a cluster of young trees, looking around frantically for some clue or sign of which way to go.

"This way." Elle pointed towards a two story, wood sided house that stood above the others.

We crept quickly through the yards, avoiding the open areas as much as possible. Coming to the back door of the two-story home, I tried the knob, and found it locked tight. Elle motioned for us to move around to the front side.

"This seems familiar." Elle smiled, stepping up onto the front porch and giving the front door knob a turn. A series of swift clicks and the door opened. Elle pushed it open and we stole inside and closed the door behind us. I leaned my back against the door, rubbed my forehead and took a deep breath.

"Where is she?" I asked when I caught my breath.

"Downstairs, just like the house you were in." She said and started making her way down the hallway, checking each door as she passed it. I joined the search but soon we were in the kitchen at the back of the home and were hit with the dismal truth.

"This isn't it," Elle said. "I'd have sworn this was the place, but this place doesn't have a basement."

"So now what?" I knew what we needed to do, which was to escape this desolate town at least until the Titan was gone, and what we morally should do, which was to find Maddie and the others.

"It was a two story house that they had her in. There can't be too many of them around this little town, right?" Elle reasoned.

"This way." I motioned for Elle to follow me. I jogged down the hallway to the front entrance where the stairway leading to the second story was. Grabbing the golden oak newel post, I spun around and leapt up onto the third step, skipping steps on the way to the upper floor. Elle followed close behind and caught me on the landing at the top of the steps.

"I'm going to check in this room, you take one of the others." I pointed to a doorway at the end of the hall.

"What are we checking for?" Elle questioned my plan.

"Look out the windows and check for other two-story homes that are close," I answered her query. "Maybe you will recognize it from up here."

With a quick nod, she ducked into the room just to her right and I hurried down the hall and into the room at the end. The room seemed to be set up as a spare bedroom. It had a full sized bed, neatly made with a tan and blue patterned bed set and more decorative pillows than anyone in their right mind would keep on their bed. A tidy dresser lined the wall near the bed and only held a family portrait in a 5"x7" frame. There were two windows, one straight ahead and one on the wall to my right. I quickly peered out of the window and searched the skyline of houses. Each block that I could see was lined with a dozen houses or more. In all, I could see nearly four blocks. My heart sank when I spotted one two-story house after another. There were, at least, two to three on each block. I turned to the other window and looked in the direction it faced. Again, I scanned the houses and found numerous two-story homes scattered throughout the neighborhood. I Stepped out into the hall to find Elle crouching on the floor in the corner between two doors.

"Get down," She whispered loudly. "It's out there." She pointed over her left shoulder towards the doorway she had entered.

"There are so many two story homes, I don't know how we are going to check them all." I squatted down and crept across the floor, getting closer and closer to my only friend in the world, Elle. A grumbling sound filled the air and an ear-splitting sound, like an exploding bomb, shook the town, shattering windows and scattering wall décor and bits of drywall across the floor.

"Come on!" I shouted. "We have to go!" My voice sounded muffled in my shell-shocked ears. Knowing Elle may not have heard me, I took her by the arm and drug her along with me, down the stairs and to the front door. Elle looked through the peephole and her face went pale. She stepped backward in disbelief and I felt her body trembling in my grasp. I refused to let her go but peeked through the peephole to see what she had been so disturbed by. The distorted view through the peephole was fish-eyed, but the vision was clear enough to shake me to my core. What was a desolate little suburban neighborhood just minutes before was now a war-torn area filled with shattered debris from houses, cars, trees and shrubs. An army of Takers wandered aimlessly through the street and yards before us. In the midst of the destruction, only a few blocks away, was the front appendage and foot of the midnight blue Titan. We rushed to the back of the home and when we found the back door, we paused.

"Now what?" I asked Elle for some glimmer of an idea that might give us some hope.

"We have two choices." Her eye flitted back and forth, looking down to the floor. "We can stay here, take our chances of not being found, and hope they just move through... or we can make a break for it, run out the back and hope we aren't spotted right away. The sun being up may help since I think they sense heat more than movement."

"I think we run." I listened to my gut instinct. "But which way do we go?"

"We go whatever way we can get away, and if we make it, we start heading west again. The desert was east, so we don't want to go that way. I guess we could go south, but west feels right." Elle sorted out her thoughts as she spoke.

I did not try to reason with her or rationalize her choice. I trusted her... with my life. I placed my finger to my lips in the universal symbol for "shhh" and reached for the back door knob. Unlocking it first, I twisted the knob and slowly pulled the door wide open. There were no Takers in our sight, it seemed like a clear path between us and the sparse tree line that lay no more than thirty yards away. I looked Elle straight in the eye and gave her a nod. Hand in hand, I turned to run out the door, but she hesitated, pulling me back. I turned back to see what was holding her back and she grabbed my mess of hair in her hand and kissed my mouth with a hard, wet and passion filled kiss.

"For luck... and just in case," She said releasing me. I could say nothing, but merely nodded again and pulled her along behind me as I exited the rear of the house.

Elle and I sprinted from the back of the house toward the tree line without ever looking back. I lost grip of her hand but did not slow down until I had passed into the trees. The patch of trees was shallower than I had expected and once within its cover, I could see the clearing on the other side. I stopped in the middle of the small piece of woods and turned to see Elle immediately behind me. We stood still for a moment catching our breath and wondering what our next move would be.

"You know, we have nothing, right?" Elle whispered intermittently through her heavy breathing. "Not even a bottle of water."

"We have each other." I tried to distract her from our destitute situation.

"Well, I'm not much on cannibalism, but if the need arises, I suppose you can... eat me." Her sarcastic innuendo made me smile inside, but it didn't help the current state of affairs.

CHAPTER 12

INTO THE TITAN

We looked around at our current surroundings to get our bearing. The sun was climbing higher in the sky, and the Titan had not moved from where its 'foot' had landed in the center of the little burb called Barnhill. Elle looked up through the tree canopy and studied the direction of the sun.

"The town is west of us, and that's the way we should go." She pointed out.

"So, maybe we go south and skirt around the town until we can travel west again." I offered up an idea.

"That sounds like the best plan to me too." Elle agreed, even though we knew we wouldn't last more than a few days with no food, water, or means to defend ourselves.

A wind grew from nothing and rustled through the branches overhead, breaking the near silence that surrounded us. When the breeze died down, the rustling of leaves remained, but instead of coming from the branches overhead, the rustling came from behind us. I spun around quickly to find a hoard of takers lead by an Ahsusha, closing in on us. Neither of us screamed 'run' out loud, but I was thinking it so loud, that I believe she heard my thoughts. We both took off running wildly through the thin stretch of woods. I ran the length of the woods instead of popping out on the other side where I would be exposed and easily found and captured.

My feet flew across the leaf litter that covered the floor of the woods and as I jutted in and out of the trees and brambles, I tried to catch a glimpse of Elle behind me as I ran, but I had lost her in the chaos. A small drop, not more than a couple of feet, caught me off guard and I tumbled down a small hill. Regaining my composure at the bottom, I heard the rushing Takers approaching, but saw no sign of Elle. I prayed that she had gotten away, but my heart knew that was unlikely.

I had a sudden memory of my last encounter with the Takers. They hadn't paid attention to me in the woods, and I had even followed them for a distance. Finding myself utterly alone, I had nothing to lose, and turned toward Barnhill and slowly walked out of the woods. The earth began to rumble again as the midnight blue Titan's appendages began to fold against themselves and the body of the mechanical giant landed flat against the earth, crushing several blocks of Barnhill and sending a shockwave across the ground that nearly knocked me to my knees. When the tremor settled, I began to wander closer to the interstellar beast. Watching the multitudes of Takers assembling and moving to the Titan, I followed them. I soon found myself surrounded by dozens of Takers and several Ahsusha.

What was I doing? I had no rational explanation for my actions, but I felt drawn to the giant craft, and I thought that if Elle or any of the others had been taken, I might be able to find them. Helping them might not be possible, but if I searched the Takers and didn't find them, perhaps that would mean they had escaped. A mechanical groaning sound bellowed through the air and I saw a small opening appear at the front of the Titan and the Ashusha escorted the Takers on board the mechanical monstrosity. I tried to decide if I could simply watch them load up and hopefully move on, or if the Ahsusha would notice if I stayed behind. While I toyed with the idea, I felt my feet moving me closer and closer to the opening. There was a desire to find the pale Titan, and perhaps this Titan would lead me to it. I had promised Elle that I would not leave her, but I did not know if she was in the crowd of Takers that had loaded into this Titan, or if she had escaped them and was in hiding. Without knowing for sure, I had to assume she had been taken and being completely unnoticed, I filed into the belly of the beast along with the others.

It was dark in the large gathering area where we stood, but being able to see better in the dimmest of lights gave me an advantage over the rest of the Takers, but not the Ahsusha. A moment of anxiety filled my senses and twisted my stomach when the door began to close. The Ahsusha escorted the Takers in groups of ten, or so, through an arched opening at the far end of the room. I wondered where they were being taken to, and had a feeling I would know soon. As the room began to empty, I noticed one of the Ahsusha was fixated on me, and I was beginning to feel that my plan to sneak on board was a secret that was known by another and perhaps I was allowed to 'sneak' on intentionally. Had the alien beings caught me by simply letting me believe that I had gone unnoticed? Clever, if that was their game, but what were their plans for me now that I was captive inside of their Titan, with no means of escape?

Aside from a pair of brightly glowing eyes, this Ahsusha, like all of them, appeared to be just another person. A tall woman, easily approaching six foot, with radiantly smooth skin like porcelain and flowing white hair, not blonde, but actually white. She wore a pair of black yoga style pants, black high top canvas sneakers and a royal-purple oversized button-down shirt that hung down to her mid-thigh. As she approached me, I noticed another Ahsusha, a man in his mid-thirties of average build and height, dressed in blue jeans, brown leather hiking boots and a plain blue long-sleeved t-shirt. The man had dark brown hair that was thinning on top and a full beard and mustache. The two moved in my direction without aggression and though I wanted to remain undercover, I remained still and waited for them to make contact. The other remaining Ahsusha escorted the remaining Takers from the area and left the three of us alone.

When the two were mere feet from me, I felt a warm sensation flooding over me, a lucidity that I hadn't known before. The woman reached out to me, laying her left thumb on my cheek, moving it with precision to find just the right placement, and her index finger on my temple, she spoke to me within my mind, without moving her emotionless lips or uttering a sound.

'I am Lori, and this is Mitch. We have awaited your return. Ornan, the commander of this vessel will be pleased that you have come. Your assistance will help us find the Pale One. The rogue 'Titan', as your people have called them, has come here to collect you. Though its commander, Moro-Dan, has a connection to your thoughts, he cannot locate you without your participation. We have followed Moro-Dan to this world and with your help, we will stop the rebellious plan he is trying to initiate.' Her voice in my head was as sweet and smooth as silk and honey, and it filled me with a comfort that took away my worries.

'Why me? And what is his rebel plan?' My thoughts were blunt but to the point.

'Moro-Dan traveled across the dimensions to connect with you on several occasions throughout your life, planting a blueprint of his plans deep within your mind, altering it as needed with each visit. He was creating an ally that would help his cause... his rebellious plan. This world was a part of our plan ever since we discovered its variety of life and elements. Our plan was simple. Come to your world when the time was right and overtake the physical bodies of your kind. We have become beings of energy and light, intelligent and conscious of ourselves. We had lost our need of true physical forms which had always been weak and vulnerable, wearing down and failing. The one thing that we lack, that you have the capability of is reproduction. Though in our current form of existence, we are nearly immortal, we cannot pro-

create and that has become the one thing we have grown to desire. Moro-Dan would have your kind rebel against us by joining with him and those with his Pale Titan to fight against our peaceful overtaking.' I absorbed every word as if I already knew exactly what she spoke of, not simply word-for-word, but the entire concept.

'And I am to help you and Ornan find this rogue Titan and stop the rebel cause? How am I to help?' I was unsure what I could do, but I felt like I was truly meant to be a part of this story. I had some important part to play, but what of Elle, and Maddie... and my life before them?

The male looked back and forth between us, as if he wondered what our conversation was filled with.

'We will take you to Ornan at the control center of the Titan, and there you will be understand more.' She removed her thumb and finger and our telepathic connection was broken. The two turned and began to walk away. I felt that I had to follow, and it was more than a need to understand, but a destiny. This was something that I was a part of, and whether I went, or fought against them and was able to escape, I was still connected to this monumental event.

Lori and Mitch turned away from me and I noticed the space where we stood had changed. There were no doorways, no corners, and no lights. I supposed that lights may have no purpose for these beings... but this was not what I would have expected. In my head I always thought of a UFO as being filled with flashing lights doors that 'swooshed' open and closed when they were approached. I followed them a dozen steps or so to an area where I noticed the floor was no longer perfectly smooth like everything else. We had stopped, and were standing in a place where the floor was covered in perfectly round, tiny bumps. There was a slight fluttering in my stomach and a growing sense of electricity in the air, like static making my hairs stand on end. There was an uncomfortable pressure in my eyes that made my vision go blurry, and a shooting pain deep within my skull. Something felt wrong and my feeling of tranquility quickly turned to uncontrollable anxiety. The other two looked at me with confusion, as I grabbed my head in my hands, afraid it might literally explode. Lori and Mitch closed their glowing eyes and dissipated right before my blurred sight. The feeling of static electricity hummed and pulsated and I thought it would kill me, but it didn't.

I felt hollow and queasy. The desire to collapse and pass out overtook me and I felt that uneasy adrenaline rush... the kind that clears your sinuses when you tip back in your chair and you almost go too far but catch yourself. Little, brilliant stars swam in the blackness of my vision for an instant before my sight returned and I found myself crumpling to the floor. Lori and Mitch stood over me, their glowing eyes stared down on me from expressionless faces. A bright glow lit their silhouettes from behind and grew closer as I regained my composure.

An alien being, Ornan, I assumed, split the two and approached. It's gelatinous, glowing figure took on the basic form of a human, though not complete. The faceless figure came close to where I sat on the floor. It lowered itself to my level, not bending or stooping, but melting its form to a shorter and thicker body. It stretched out its arms to me, reaching for my head with its chubby-jello fingers. Lightning struck, metaphorically, when it touched the sides of my head, I felt its energy penetrating my brain and filling it with a myriad of information. In a split second, the being broke contact and an audible screeching moan echoed through the hollow space. Its form stretched and twisted in what appeared to be a very unnatural way. The alien glow of its energy dimmed and flickered, leaving a puddled blob that slowly shrank and evaporated in our presence.

CHAPTER 13

HOMELESS

I stood up and felt good. There was confusion, a feeling that I was not remembering everything that was important to me, but I didn't feel sick; I wasn't dizzy; my body did not ache in the slightest. I felt... complete. In the moment I stood, the Titan shook and groaned a terrible mechanical groan. The giant shuddered and I could sense that it was taking a stand though it felt different than I had expected, more labored and less powerful. A sense of control filled my being, but the glow in Lori and Mitch's eyes dimmed as they stepped back. My mind was overloaded with thoughts and ideas that were not my own, but my body... *my body*... was suddenly filled with an energy that made me feel physically complete. The two Ahsushas, Lori, and Mitch seemed intimidated and almost afraid of me. They lowered their eyes and would not look directly at me.

The limitless thoughts in my head flashed like a slideshow of pictures I did not remember. Some of the thoughts were ideas of internal workings of the Titan, and how and where it was controlled. Other flickers of thought were of the armies of Takers that were held in the belly of the titan. Each thought had a million other ideas and memories attached to it and it was more than my brain could comprehend. There was a surprising picture, like a short clip from an old home-movie, that flashed in the midst of all of the alien knowledge... A raven haired woman, tan and fit, squatted down in a dimly lit cave. Her expression was blank, but there was a kindness in her dark eyes. I knew this person held some importance, but I could not place who she was, or what role she had played.

"Will you find the rogue Titan, now... Ornan?" Lori spoke aloud, and her voice was feminine but raspy as if she had not used it in a very long time.

"I seek the Pale Titan, and I seek a woman with ebony hair and dark skin from my memory. I will find them both if I am able...." My words came without thought but sounded foreign to me. "Ornan exists no more. I am Tanner. I have always been Tanner, and I will remain Tanner."

The moment I decided that I desired to find the rogue Pale Titan, the mechanical giant we were inside of began to move, stretching one appendage at a time, and slamming hard into the earth below with each step. Lori and Mitch backed aside a few steps, opening a pathway and extending their arms as if to say 'this way'. I knew without question, that I should follow the way before me. As I approached the edge of the rounded room, things that were unseen became visible. There were a series of windows, a wall full of them in fact. These were not the typical windows that

I had been accustomed to. Though I could not remember much of my past, I had flashes of memory, and those flashes were confusing and felt out of place. All the same, these windows seemed unusual in that they were not pieces of clear elements framed to fill openings in a wall. The wall itself simply became clear in a large area, revealing a panoramic view from a height that was almost dizzying.

Although the entire 'plan' was buried in my brain, I had not taken the time to think it through. My only concern for the moment was to find the rogue, Pale Titan, and the majestic Titan that I rode seemed on a set course to find it. Somehow my thoughts and desires were controlling this giant. I wondered if normal people were scattering below. In the moment that the thought entered my head, a series of infra-red lights began to glow red from just below the 'window' and the earth below was suddenly a mixture of the normal color and light spectrum and infra-red to ultraviolet that showed heat signatures. Despite being more than three hundred feet in the air, I could plainly see the movements of the smallest of mammals: squirrels, rabbits, birds, and mice. A human or a group of them would be blatantly unmistakable... easy targets.

The Titan strode over the countryside in long and purposeful steps and my mind shifted to misplaced memories. While this monstrous, mechanical gorilla remained on course to find the rogue Titan, I scoured my mind in search of lost bits of my humanity. Flashes of being on a jet plane that was about to crash, coming to consciousness in the desert alone, being rescued by a mysterious person shrouded in black, a gathering of people in a comfortable living room and a beautiful woman by my side... Raven black hair, deep and thoughtful eyes that drew me in, dark tanned skin... I knew this woman. She was my companion, my savior... my lover... A dark and mysterious scene played out in the corridors of my mind; this powerful and beautiful woman was seductively and submissively intertwined with me, flesh on flesh, hot breath on hyper-sensitive skin, need and desire exchanged between her and me, and passion and pleasure unequaled... ELLE!

In that moment, I knew. I knew... everything, or, at least, I suddenly remembered everything, and the rogue, pale Titan was no longer as important to me as this woman that I had promised I would never leave... this woman that I... was in love with. With a vertiginous spin, the Titan turned. A few steps, a few miles, and we were headed back to where we had just come from, which told me that somehow the Titan knew, I knew, that Elle was alive and she had escaped the army of Takers.

Like a drunken sailor, the Titan stumbled when its front leg stepped over the edge of a small ravine. This step should have been easily maneuvered, but the Titan seemed to be losing control. My purpose was split. There was a need to find the rogue Titan that I did not fully understand, and a desire to find Elle, that I could not deny. My confusion was feeding into the central controls of the beast and my emotions confounded its programming. Emotion had never played a part, and the previous commander of the Titan had only directed it with a meticulous, apathetic purpose. Two more shaky steps, like those of a fawn just learning to walk, and the Titan came crashing down, its four tremendous appendages folding under itself. I rode the falling Titan like a surfer in an aerial, dropping in and catching an a-frame wave, while the two Ahsushas, Lori, and Mitch, tumbled to the floor.

I traveled across the command room, which now appeared as a simple gray room, round and nondescript. I knew what I wanted. I wanted to leave the Titan and find Elle, and as simple as that, there was an odd vibration, and a darkening of my sight, and I found myself heading towards a brightly lit opening. Passing through the light, my feet found the grass covered ground beneath them.

Forward, I pressed on, through a forest valley, without looking back for nearly twenty minutes. The trees were plentiful and varied. Twisted Coast Live Oaks, Cedars, Thorn Apples and Cottonwoods filled the forest with a diversity that I found beautiful in the most profound way. The trees did not judge each other by their height or their specific genus or species. They lived in harmony, side by side, each one absorbing the sun and never jealous or even noticing which tree had the longest branches, the most leaves or which photosynthesized the most efficiently. They merely existed together... and together in that way, they were brilliant.

I began to think about the two Ahsushas, and all of the Takers that I had left behind in the Titan. What had become of them? Though we had different purposes and reasons for being, we were basically the same. If it were not for the desire to overpower, we would be basically the same: beings that wanted to exist for our own peace and happiness. Finally, I turned to see the Titan where it had crumpled to the earth and I was taken aback.

The Titan that I had boarded sneakily had been a deep midnight blue. I watched as it now appeared a very pale blue, even lighter than the sky. It faded as I watched and soon was an ashy white color, as if all of its power, all of its life was fading from it. As shocking as this was, I was more concerned by what I saw between the white Titan and me... Lori and Mitch were leading a troupe of Takers, and they seemed to be following me. Though they were quite a distance behind and I wasn't really able to see the two leading them, I could sense it. It was more like watching masses of ants moving very slowly in my direction. I really had no real idea of where I was, and I could only trust my instinct as to which way I should go.

There were three things that I knew... three things that seemed most important to me...

1) I had to find my way back to Elle.

2) I had to find out what had happened to little Maddie.

3) I had to find my way home.

I had a feeling if I found the first two, I would have to look no further to find the third.

While I walked swiftly uphill, I wondered what would become of the Ahsushas and the Takers without a 'commander' and a functioning Titan to sustain them. *'Don't follow me. Why couldn't you just stay there with the Titan?'* I thought out loud, wishing that for once, I could not constantly worry about being chased or sought out by an army of drones. Climbing out of the valley and reaching the apex of the ravine, I turned to look over my shoulder. There, at the farthest point of the vale, laid the Titan, like a hunter's trophy. The Takers and Ahsushas stood, gathered in a huddled mass at the base of the lifeless monstrosity, staring up, in my direction. I could feel them watching me, watching my every step, but no longer following me. I stood looking down at them, and much to my surprise I began to hear a sound. It sounded like a synchronized vocalization... slow and deliberate. I listened as the sound repeated and knew that somehow it came from the Takers below though I had never heard any of them utter a single sound. The coordinated voice was like the sound of a distant crowd at a sporting event, calling out together, but without the energetic passion. At first, I could not make out the rhythmic chant. But the longer I listened, the clearer it became...

"U-NI-FY..."

The word repeated and echoed through the valley. My first thoughts were of the troupe of Takers, banding together under the authority of the Ahsushas, Lori, and Mitch, but I began to come to an understanding... a lucid knowledge that what they were chanting was a desire for what I had become. I had not been overcome by the Ahsusha to become a Taker; I had not become an Ahsusha when touched by the Titan commander. On a level that I did not yet understand, and for a reason that would someday make devastating sense to me, I had become a blend of alien and human.

I was a unique Convergence.

Convergence: v. 1. When two or more things come together to form a new whole. 2. two or more things coming together, joining together, or evolving into one. 3. The coming together of two or more distinct entities or phenomenon.

The Genesis Project

Chapter 1

The Road Less Traveled

The seemingly mindless chanting of the Takers echoed in my head and throughout the forest, hauntingly. Standing at the precipice of the ravine, the brilliant ball of fire, we call the sun, was passed midday. I had lost track of time. It seemed like only a few hours since I had slipped on board the Titan, but the more I thought about all of the information in my head and everything that had happened, everything that had changed... it could have been days or even weeks. Each physical encounter with an Ahsusha, or alien being, had resulted in a loss of memory and a period of complete confusion. With no one and nothing to relate time to, I was lost.

I was not only lost in time, I was physically lost. How far we had traveled in the Titan was a mystery and I could only hope that I could find Barnhill again. I did not know if Elle would be there if Maddie would be there and be okay, or even alive, but... it was the last place I knew they had been. I had to find my way back there, if for no other reason, to begin my search for them. The decision to retrace the path of the Titan was my best bet to find the town, but it was sort of a shot in the dark. The Titan could have wandered for days, zigzagging across the wilderness. Barnhill could be less than a few miles away as the crow flies, but the Titan's path might have traveled dozens or even hundreds of miles. I began to feel overwhelmed and uncertain of my path. The one thing that I was certain of... I was starving.

I left the chanting hoard behind me and followed what appeared to be the path of the Titan. I searched the sparse forest for anything that seemed edible. There were no berry bushes, no nut trees that I could find and I thought about the odds of trapping a hare, of finding a lizard or turtle... I had no way to start a fire. Depression began to set in. A drink of lemonade and one of those dry cereal bars... I would kill for a bite of one of Elle's dry cereal bars. Pains in my stomach poked at me like dull knives tearing at my insides. Nearly a full day of walking had left me no closer to finding any sustenance and my anxiety and psychological state had left me feeling that I may be no closer to finding my one true friend.

As the tormenting sun began to sink lower in the sky on my second day of walking, dying from starvation seemed more likely than ever finding my way back. Sitting on a hard slab of sandstone, with my head in my hands, the voices in my head argued. A weak and timid persona swayed me to believe that giving up, curling up, and waiting to die was inevitable. Another more commanding voice told me to fill my stomach with anything, even dirt, and grasses, to ease the pain, but to never give up because I had a greater purpose... I would have never made it this far if I did not. A twisted conifer wrapped itself around me like it was hugging me, or shielding me though its spindly form was far from comforting or protective. My body, weak and exhausted, crumpled over on the hard slab and I drifted off to a delirious slumber.

Several hours of uninterrupted sleep had passed when I heard a familiar voice.

"Hey you... Wake up... you need to eat something." The voice of Elle filled my head with comfort. How she managed to find me in the middle of the wilderness, I had no idea, but I knew she was right.

"Elle..." I groaned sleepily, trying to clear my blurry, waking vision.

"Eat something... anything... baby." Her hand reached out to me and she ran her fingers through my hair and leaned in, sniffing my cheek... and then licking it.

I awoke with a start from a dream that I wished, more than anything, had been real. The stars filled the night sky and the sliver of a moon smiled down on my desperate situation. 'Sniff-

sniff'. I flinched and my head spun to the side. There, laying nuzzled up beside me was a full grown golden retriever... not an old dog, but no pup either.

"Where did you come from?" I asked out loud as if this canine would somehow answer me back. He did answer in his own way. He sat up and his tail wagged vigorously.

A smile broke across my face, despite the wrenching cramps in my empty gut. Leaning on one hand, I rubbed his head with my free hand, scratching his yellow fur and floppy ears. He seemed quite content to have found a companion. While I petted and stroked his coat, I began to notice movement nearby. This was not the movement of wandering Takers, or even a random deer or coyote. What I was noticing was a flurry of insects scavenging around on the forest floor. Elle's words haunted my thoughts... *Eat something... anything'.* A primal instinct took over and I began to gasp at the tiny movements and quickly began shoving crickets, beetles and anything I could grab, into my mouth, crunching and squishing their disgusting shells and guts as if they were delicacies as if my life depended on it... which it did.

When I could no longer force myself to devour any more of the foul bugs, I peeled a small patch of moss from the base of the twisted cedar and began to chew on it to clear my mouth of the repulsive taste and feel of the insect bits and pieces that remained lodged, with nothing to wash it all down with. Much to my surprise and pleasure, the moss held a considerable amount of moisture and also caused my mouth to water. The retriever sat and eagerly watched as I fed myself on insects and the clumps of moss.

I reached up and rubbed his neck, feeling for a collar. A wide, nylon, green and blue, weaved collar had been buried and hidden beneath his thick and matted coat. Both hands took hold of it and my fingers searched the collar. A jingling sound was like music to my ears. It is quite amazing how much the smallest of things can bring a smile and satisfaction when you have nothing. The jingle came from two dog tags that dangled from the well-worn collar and I slipped the collar to the side, in order to get a better look at the tags. The first was an official silver tag and let me know that the pooch had been well cared for and was up to date on his shots. The second was a metallic yellow-colored tag and held the information I had hoped for. His home was on Joshua Lane in Barnhill, his name was Josie, and *'he'* was a she. The best news was the name of the town, Barnhill. Dogs have been known to wander from one side of the country to the other, but perhaps Josie would lead me back to her home.

I was feeling a bit rested, and although a bit queasy, my hunger pangs were tolerable. It was hours before sunrise, but I was no longer concerned about running into any Takers or Titans. I stood up and Josie perked up, jumping up on me, bouncing on her back feet excitedly. I ruffled her ears and head in my hands and put my nose right up to her cold and wet nose.

"Hey Josie girl!" I spoke to her as if I were speaking to a very young child or a dog of my own, in an energy-filled voice that wasn't really mine. "You wanna go home? Come on girl, let's go home."

Josie jumped up and licked me square on the mouth, and her butt wiggled and her tail wagged in a most feverish way. Though I had no idea of the exact direction, I took a couple of steps to the east, in the same direction I had been traveling the day before. Josie trotted ahead a few paces, but then stopped abruptly and turned to see if I was following behind. When I caught up with her, I patted her side and stroked her coat. Josie panted and looked straight into my glowing eyes without fear or question. This dog had befriended a total stranger, simply on the basis that I was willing to be kind to her and be her friend too.

The remainder of the night, and most of the next day continued in much the same way: Josie running ahead and then waiting for me to catch up. She instinctively knew where the best and safest paths were and it felt, to me, as if we were headed in the right direction. Without warning, after catching up to Josie just an hour or so before the sun began to set on our first day together, she nuzzled my hand with her head and nose and took off to our right, at a ninety-degree angle from the direction we had been heading. I wondered if she had been distracted by a small animal or scent, and I began to worry that maybe she was just wandering through the forest in no particular direction.

She darted out of my sight but soon came rushing back. Josie circled me twice, and jumping up, pawed at me... whimpering to get my attention.

"Get down girl..." I said in my doggie-talk voice. "You're gonna get me all muddy." A sudden wave of excitement poured over me and hope tingled throughout my body. Josie's paws were muddy, and muddy paws meant... water! "Let's go Josie girl! Let's go!" Somehow I found a surge of hidden energy and I nearly ran after her, through a briar thicket and up a small hill. On my descent down the other side, I watched and literally teared up when I saw Josie galloping down the hill and then leap into a small stream that ran between two spoil-bank hills. She splashed and frolicked in the shallow water and I felt as if I could splash right along with her... I felt as if she may have just saved my life.

I bolted down the hill faster than my feet could carry me. Two-thirds of the way down, my momentum overtook my coordination. I tumbled forward with my feet flying up behind me, my right shoulder and the side of my face planting and then dragging through the leaves and sticks that covered the forest floor. I completed my tumble with my back pounding hard against the hillside, knocking the wind out of me as I slid down the remainder of the hill. Twigs and exposed roots scraped my shoulders, neck, and back, and the back of my skull and my ear were scratched and bleeding when I came to rest at the bottom, against a young sapling. Pain and anger washed over me but quickly vanished when Josie trotted up, licking my face, whimpering, and dripping creek-water on me. I quickly recovered my composure and though I was cut up, bruised and sore, I managed to regain my footing, sauntered over to the stream and knelt down over it. I dipped my hands in the cool running water and raised them to my face as if saying a prayer and giving thanks to mother earth.

I cupped my hands and scooped up the crystal clear water, drinking up as much as I could contain. The cool water trickled between my tightly closed fingers, spattering the creek like raindrops and running down my forearms to my elbows. I had been given hope by man's best friend. This was the second time since the appearance of the Titans that I had been saved by a female... first Elle, and now Josie. Elle... a picture of her face, and the feeling of holding her intimately close, was burned into my memory.

Alien invaders, zombie-like Takers, hybrid Ahsushas, and my own strange adaptation and mixture of alien traits... not to mention this feeling that I was an intentional pivot point of some type of revolution... and yet for some reason, Elle was the thing that filled my thoughts. She had become not only the most important thing in my world... in only a few short weeks, she had become my world.

After filling my belly with cool stream water, and watching Josie playing so contently, I pulled my long sleeved t-shirt (that used to be white) over my head and kicked off my shoes. Unbuttoning and unzipping the blue jeans that Elle had found for me, I shimmied them off. The stream was only a couple of feet wide and less than a foot deep, but it was the closest thing to a bath I had and the cool running water was exhilarating as it rushed over my parched and overheated skin. I knelt in the creek, naked and exposed for all of nature to see, and rinsed my clothes in its swift flowing beauty. I sat in the water, splashing myself and soaking up the life-giving element.

Standing up, I began to awkwardly don my sopping wet clothes. The jeans seemed to weigh a ton and even though they were uncomfortably soaked, I knew they would probably dry out all too quickly. I pulled the long-sleeved, cotton t-shirt back over my head, and the neck stretched out unnaturally. Putting the jeans on was difficult, but the dripping wet shirt was nearly impossible. It clung to me like sticky-tape and I felt like a child who was learning to dress himself for the first time. When I finally had it on, it hung loosely and seemed over-sized, which made me feel even more childlike. Josie played and splashed downstream and lapped up as much water as she could hold. After over an hour of fluid bliss, I slipped on my shoes and called out to my new traveling companion.

"Come on girl, let's go home," I said, thinking if I said a simple and possibly familiar phrase, she might understand in the way dogs understand basic verbal commands. I had no doubt that dogs, and many animals, understood emotions and physical cues. Josie jumped into action with my words and that gave me hope that she recognized something I had said, and I had hopes that if there was only one word that she was reacting to, that word was *home*.

We trekked along as the sunset turned the sky from an unremarkable pale blue palette, dotted with puffy cotton balls, to a canvas covered in a dozen shades of oranges, reds, and purples as if Monet himself had painted it with blurry watercolors, that began to show more and more through the treetops as the forest thinned out. I tried to keep the thin ribbon of the stream in my view as long as I could, but after a few hours of night, we had drifted too far left of where it had trickled through the almost mountainous woods.

The days in the desert had been searing, and in this forest, they had been smotheringly sultry, but the night was quickly growing cool, and my clothes were still slightly on the damp side. I longed for a fire, and a bed and blanket... and Elle. While we journeyed, I searched for a resting spot, but no real shelter could be found. When the sky had darkened and pinpoints of starlight speckled the evening sky, we began to pass through a grove of evergreens. This patch of pines was denser than the sparse woods we had been wandering through and the thick layer of dead pine needles felt soft underfoot. I chose this spot to spend the night and Josie quickly agreed. Nearly laying on the ground, I used the entire length of my arms and hands to scoop the thick layer of needles into a large pile, a few feet wide, over six feet in length and nearly eight inches thick. Though it took quite some time, I didn't mind; I had nothing else to do. Josie sat nearby, watching intently and I worked. When I had finished, I glanced over at her and her big dark eyes had the most pitiful look. I felt a little guilty, so I started scooping up more needled together to make another spot for her. I made her bedding in a circular shape, about three foot across and almost as thick as what I had made for myself. When I was finished, I looked over and saw her sitting with her mouth open, tongue hanging out, appearing to smile if that were a possibility... I had been played by a retriever.

"There you go girl." I gently whispered as I patted the palette of pine needles. Josie stood up, slowly stepped up onto her bed and after turning three full circles, laid down. Tucking her nose under her tail, she turned into a dirty yellow furball. I sat down next to her and petted her soft coat, and let myself unwind for a few minutes before lying down. A flurry of thoughts spun recklessly in my head as I sat quietly: pictures of Elle and I carelessly goofing around, little Maddie's quest for a peanut-butter sandwich, a mental and physical connection with the Titan, the chanting of the Takers, a night of confusion and awakening in a vast desert, the death of Bobby...

When the thoughts slowed and my mind's worry eased, I worked my way into my own pile of pines, laid down, and thought of days gone by and futures that might have been as I slipped away to a peaceful dreamland...

It was a crisp and early morning, just before sunrise. I wandered down an empty street in a large, deserted city. The view was as cold and empty as the winter air that nipped at my nose and stung my ears. The chill was the only thing that even touched my senses. The silence was deafening and not even the sound of wind could be heard. There was no smell of car exhaust or breakfast cooking at a sidewalk bistro. It seemed a dead and barren, urban wasteland. Turning the gray, concrete corner, my footsteps stopped abruptly. Towering over the city, a blackish-blue Titan seemed to stare down at me. Anxiety filled my stomach with knots and butterflies, and as I watched the Titan fade from the darkest blue imaginable to a pale chalky white, the sound of church bells rang out from a different direction than the Titan.

Like a lab rat in a maze, searching for the chunk of cheddar at the finish line, I took off in search of the bells. Running down the streets, turning corners in hopes of finding the source before the melodic ringing ended, I felt like I was trapped in some lost episode of The Twilight Zone. A cold sweat beaded on my forehead and dampened my upper lip. I zipped around the corner of an older brick building. The echoing shock of the last ringing of the bells, and the sight of a Gothic-looking, limestone cathedral filled me with awe. Its steeple, crowned with a copper cross, tarnished and green from exposure, towered over the skyline. I slowed to a cautious walk when I climbed the weather-stained steps. A set of immense, ornate wooden doors lay before me and swung open effortlessly before I could even reach for them.

I stepped through the entryway like I was stepping through some mystical portal. Breezing through the vestibule and into the sanctuary, I found pews filled with people of all shapes, sizes, ages... every race, creed, and color... A long line had formed up the center aisle as if waiting their turn for 'Holy Communion'. I turned my gaze to where the pastor or priest should be, but instead, there was a man in everyday, street clothes, bent over to the young woman in front of him. His face was hidden from my view by the full, jet black hair of the woman at the front of the line. When she had finished, she turned to return down the aisle. The blood ran from my face and I felt faint when I saw her glowing eyes.

"ELLE!" I cried out in disbelief.

Everyone in the congregation and the line turned to look at me. My knees went weak and I trembled all over when I watched the sea of glowing eyes land their stares directly on me, with their arms outstretched. The man at the head of the line, where the pastor should have been stood up straight and tall, dropping the chalice from his hand and blood poured from it, splattering and spilling out on the floor beneath it. His dazed look was only surpassed by my own when I looked into his glowing eyes and met my own reflection, my face... it was me. The scene went blood red and then black.

The dream ended, but I managed to sleep a while longer until a wriggling stirred me. More than half asleep, I rolled onto my side and wrapped my arm around Josie. I buried my frosty face in the back of her neck and soaked up her warmth for another hour, trying to wake up, trying to remember and process the frighteningly, realistic dream.

Please leave us a review if you enjoyed the read

More Books by Rick Kueber

The Convergence Saga continues...

The Genesis Project

Dissention (Summer 2016)

Best Sellers in Supernatural in Paperback and Kindle

Frost and Flame Trilogy

Forever Ash: The Witch Child of Helmach Creek

Shadows of Eternity: The Children of the Owls

Neverending Maddness: A Girl Lost to the World

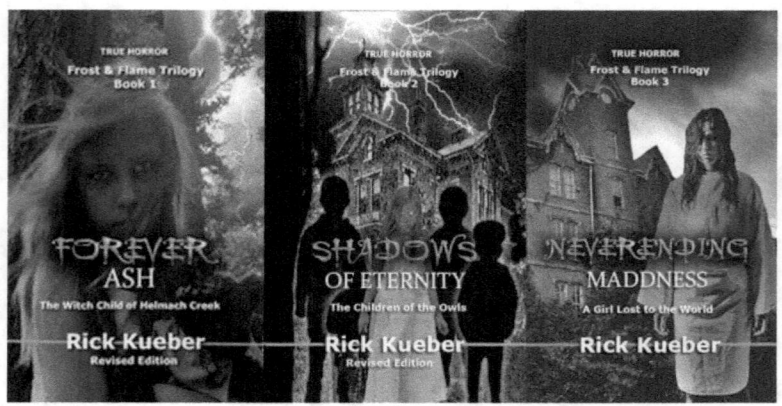

More From Stellium Books

Amazon #1 Best Seller in Supernatural

Top 20 Best Seller since October 2015.

Amazing Paranormal Encounters Volume 1

Amazing Paranormal Encounters Volume 2

(February 2016)

www.ingramcontent.com/pod-product-compliance
Lightning Source LLC
Chambersburg PA
CBHW070018260626
47159CB00005B/1859